The Newcomer

Twelve Science Fiction Short Stories

edited by Alasdair Shaw

First published 2016
ISBN10 0995511012
ISBN13 978-0995511019

Contents

Introduction

This collection of short stories was put together to showcase the variety of talented authors writing science fiction today. The twelve chosen come from around the world, including the US, Britain, Canada, Taiwan, and China.

Each tale presented here explores the central theme of an arrival by someone or something new. And the reactions produced range, as they often do, from hope to fear.

#

The world is nothing but a dry husk of itself. Jacob Heinlein has lost his home, everyone he knew, and hope. While on a journey to the mythical ocean, an unforgiving sun beating down on him, Jacob finds himself in a town with a source of fresh, clean water. However, there is a "Tithe" to pay for the privilege of staying.

In "Exodus", the orphaned children of Old Earth are scattered across the solar system, protected from the darkness by god-like beings fashioned from lost technologies. But something has changed. Ancient rules have been broken, and after centuries of isolation one of these beings approaches Mars with overtly hostile intent. A defence must be marshalled, and the coming conflagration could result in the destruction of one of the last bastions of man.

Humanity had aimed for the stars and a glorious future in space. The alien's arrival had tarnished that shiny dream. Now the first AIs are fully coming online, even while the government tries to block their use, and humanity is once again looking to the future. "First Bonding" tells of the illegally-created level 8 AI known as Genghis, and his reactions to an alien attack.

In "Ice Dreamer", lab technician Prussis has dreamed all her life of reviving someone from the past. Whilst no-one understands why she keeps trying, she works long hours defrosting heads. In her latest attempt, what happens is the last thing she expects.

Then in "The Nanny", the first natural birth in over two hundred years brings a new life to Cardea's family. Despite the risks, she and her husband are determined to raise a family the old fashioned way. But social habits die hard.

The war with a forgotten conqueror has been over for decades, but that doesn't mean the Earth has recovered. Life in the American Midwest is only getting more dangerous. His town besieged by hunter-killer drones left over from the conflict, gifted high school senior Daniel Bell would give his "Right Hand" to make the Army believe that the machines are somehow not being harmed by their operations.

"What Make is Your Cat?" welcomes you to London-Atlantis where, after the tsunami, your cat has higher social status and earning power than you do, and evolution is an elite, designer trend you can't afford to join.

Three-month-old Clem faces his first day of "Kaxian Duty" with anxiety. He is keen to find out what his assignment will be, but runs into distractions on the way to headquarters. Training will be hard.

Mistakes will be punished. Oh, and his tail has a mind of its own, which doesn't help matters any.

Ary had known he was destined to be a starship captain his whole life. After all, his mother was Captain Sandy and his father was the guy who was supposed to be Fleet Admiral. However, the prospect of attending the Spaceforce Academy was daunting. Enough to make Ary question his future. In his first few weeks there will be quite a few "Lessons Learned".

Bounty hunter Braillen takes a new job on "The Humra" to get close to her mark. When the crew discover her identity she is whisked in front of the captain. She must face her nightmares if she wants to finish the job and realise her deepest desire.

New captains take command in a variety of situations. Sometimes the passage isn't an easy one. In "The Hawk of Destiny's Fist", Asarik Leah is sent to replace ShipLord Till and lead his InquiryShip on a dangerous new mission. Tradition demands she proves herself fit to take his place.

And in our last story, newly-promoted Commander Olivia Johnson is posted to the destroyer "Repulse". Most of the officers are dead and the remaining crewmembers are exhausted. Johnson must step up to the mark and lead them back into battle despite her personal misgivings.

#

And so, on to the stories. I hope you enjoy...

-o-

Tithe

by Griffin Carmichael

It looked like a mirage, tempting him at the edge of his vision. The heat shimmered and baked better than any oven he'd ever seen, and the dryness of his throat was a cruel reminder that it had been nearly a week since the last trickle of water he found. He didn't have to shake the canteen hanging from his waist to know it was empty.

Jacob stood wavering in the sun, squinting. He could go forward, head to the mirage, or he could try west, and try to find the end of the desert. He vaguely remembered people talking about something called an ocean, long ago in his barely remembered youth. *Ocean* meant water. Salt water, his brain insisted. Not good. But water was water. There were ways to get the salt out. His Grandpappy had said so, long ago when he was a boy.

There would be people close to water, he knew. Maybe they would teach him how to banish the demon salt.

It looked like real buildings ahead, though. If it was a town, a Wanderer's caravan, even a group of travellers like himself, searching for a new beginning, there was a chance he could get water. Trade or work, it didn't matter. He needed water.

Jacob sighed and trudged forward. The mirage was to the south of where he wanted to be heading, but he'd followed a dry stream bed this way, hoping to find the source, a spring or pond that might hold enough precious moisture to get him further along.

#

Maybe the town was built beside a good source of water. Jacob's mind wandered as he walked towards the mirage. It didn't seem to get any closer, which made his heart thump hard in his chest. He couldn't walk much further, so tired and dry he felt like an old corn husk. He'd have to head west soon, or die here in this wasteland.

The thought of corn, sweet and moist as the boiled ear came out of the pot made him want to cry. It had been so long since he'd tasted anything so pure and good. Corn took water to grow, and as the rivers and streams and wells began to dry up, water was too precious to spare to grow corn.

It was getting hotter. Jacob rummaged in his pouch for a small stone, placing the rounded pebble under his tongue. If he was lucky, he could bring a small amount of saliva out of his squeezed-dry cells, just enough to keep him going for a little longer.

It worked, just barely, and he savored the spit as long as he could. Jacob put one worn boot in front on the other, over and over, until his mind refused to put forth coherent thought. After that, he just walked, an automaton that looked like a man.

The sun gradually shifted, until it was teasing him from the west. The right side of his body was blazing from the sun's rays striking him, which wasn't any relief from when it had rained fire down on top of his head.

Jacob took an old bandanna, threadbare and reeking of old sweat, and draped it over that side of his head. It blocked enough sun that he imagined he felt relief from the unbearable heat.

And he kept walking.

To stop now was certain death, to lie out in the sun without any shelter would surely be the last of him.

Hours passed, the sun sank deeper and deeper towards the horizon. If Jacob could have reasoned, he would have turned to walk into the golden ball, towards the mythical ocean.

But he kept walking.

Then he shuffled, too far gone to lift tired feet up and forward. It was twilight, and he imagined a cool breeze swept over his aching body. His imagination gave him a whiff of water smell. It was so dainty and light. Jacob's heart hitched, his breath caught in his chest. He could die now, with the smell of fresh, clean water filling his nose, cooling his battered skin.

It didn't matter that it was an illusion, a trick of his dying brain. It *felt* real, and that was blessing enough, to die with the scent of water perfuming his last moments.

He never noticed when he passed through the city gate, held open by men who watched him continue his slow, tortured shuffle forward. Never saw the people rushing to catch him as he fell, spent, in front of the town well.

#

He awoke with thoughts of Heaven foremost in his brain, and the sights that greeted his wavering eyesight did little to dispel that. Sunlight filtered into the room through an old wooden shutter, highlighting the plaster ceiling and walls, the few pieces of rough-hewn furniture emerging from the night's shadow.

Jacob turned his head with an effort, taking it all in. The heat and dusty air surely wouldn't be a feature of Heaven, but of the all-too-real world he knew. The disappointment caused his chest to contract painfully. He was surprised when tears wet his eyes. He hadn't been able to cry for a long time.

Damn God for leaving him on this forsaken world! What kind of loving Father would do that to His most faithful servant? Try as he might, Jacob began to believe less in that love and more in the notion that God was nothing more than a cruel, capricious bastard.

The sound of the door opening took Jacob away from his thoughts and brought his gaze to the woman who entered. She carried a tray, and her attention was focused on keeping the contents steady. She didn't notice Jacob was awake and watching her until she'd closed the door and was halfway to the cot where he lay.

"Oh, you're awake!"

Jacob nodded. "Yes. Where am I?"

His voice was little more than a croak, his throat was still so dry.

The woman stood blinking at him for a long while. She was dressed simply, in a loose, woven robe that covered her from throat to toe. Dark blonde hair was piled up on top of her head, a few fine tendrils loose and waving in a slight breeze.

Jacob thought she was the most beautiful sight he'd ever seen, especially when she finally moved to set the tray on a rickety bedside table. The cup she proceeded to fill with water and offer to him was surely the second most beautiful sight.

Jacob gulped the liquid, though he tried to make it last. It was so precious, so rare, that he wanted to savor it like the finest wine. But he was too thirsty, and so the water disappeared quickly. How astounding when the woman poured him another, and then another.

Finally, Jacob settled back against the wall and tried to speak again. This time his voice was much clearer, smoother.

"Thank you. Will you tell me, where I am? I've travelled so long, and the journey has been hard."

The woman hesitated. "I think it's best you wait for Administrator James. He will make all clear to you."

After helping Jacob with more water, the woman took up the tray and left the room. There was a small sound as the door closed, and Jacob suspected the door had been secured. He was too weak to care, and as he lay back on the clean bedding he drifted into sleep.

#

Some time later, Jacob awoke to see the room had slipped again into shadow. He could barely make out the items in the room, only the glow coming through the window and striking the white plaster made it possible. There was no candle or lantern to be seen, so he pulled himself up and waited for someone to come.

How long he waited he didn't know, but the light was fading into darkness before he heard the sound of the door being unlocked. When it swung open, the light of a lantern blinded Jacob for a moment. By the time his eyes had adjusted, a man was standing beside the bed, holding the lantern high.

The man watched Jacob, taking in his features, studying him like a bird of prey. His face was passive, no emotion breaking through.

Jacob was still, letting the man take his measure. It was to be expected, when one was a stranger. In return, Jacob studied the man. He saw graying brown hair, hazel eyes marked by wrinkles, though he thought the man not much older than himself. His skin was weathered, like everyone who lived in this harsh world.

Finally, the man smiled. Jacob couldn't help himself and smiled back.

"Welcome, stranger. You have had a long journey, we could tell when you arrived. It's taken many days until you recovered enough so I could talk with you. I am Samuel Malloy, Administrator of this community. And your name?"

"Jacob. Jacob Heinlein."

The man—an Administrator, whatever that was—laughed. "No relation, I suppose, to the long ago writer of fanciful tales? We have several of his works, preserved carefully in the Library."

Jacob shook his head. "I don't know, Administrator. My family long ago lost whatever records they had. It's just a name we knew to call ourselves in our village, handed down from father to son."

"Well, no matter. It was just a peculiar notion I had. In the world long gone, many held great stock in even distant relations to famous people. Today, it's your own good faith and work that distinguish you."

Malloy turned around, searching for something. It was only then that Jacob realized that two other men had entered the room after him. One of them pushed a small wooden chair up to the bed.

"Ah, thank you, Markus." Malloy situated the chair so he was close to Jacob's bedside, a good distance for talk but not too close.

"Now. I'm sure you have many questions. The tending woman said you'd asked where you are. Normal curiosity, but you must understand that I need to be sure of your intentions before you're given information that might be used against us. Many have tried to take our community by force."

Jacob nodded. It was the usual way of things, that those with nothing would take from those who had something, no matter how small a thing it was. To have water enough to be given freely to a stranger meant they were rich, indeed.

"So, Jacob Heinlein, might you share where you are from, and why you were travelling under such mean circumstances? We know you had nothing with you except a bag containing animal snares, a canteen, and some small articles of clothing. Your old knife was little more than a gesture towards offering any real protection.

"Which leaves me wondering, I won't deny. We see few enough travellers these days, even the rebels and renegades have begun to die out. So, what brought you to our fair community?"

Jacob swallowed, thinking hard. How much he should reveal, how much dignity he could keep for himself. He felt the blush of shame coloring his cheeks, and knew the other men could see it clearly in the bright glow of the lantern.

Malloy waited him out, head tipped to one side, a slight smile on his lips. He was settled into the little chair, as if he could and would wait a long time for Jacob to answer.

Finally, it could be put off no longer. Jacob decided to tell it all, and let the Administrator use it as he would.

"I come from far away, many months walking to the East. Once I lived in a thriving community, with a good spring and lush crops. We were happy, and content to live simply."

Malloy nodded. "As we ourselves are, here. But, go on."

"One day, we noticed that our water wasn't as plentiful as it once was, our harvests leaner. It became harder and harder to keep us all fed. We gradually decreased our livestock, changed the crops we grew, and we went on, poorer but still happy."

Jacob paused, sighing. How he dreaded telling the next part of the tale. He didn't want to share the rest with a stranger, but if it was the price to be paid for even one more cup of water, then so be it.

"We knew other villages were suffering as we were, because people talk when trading, no matter how many times the leaders say to keep our secrets our own. It was on one such trading day that something went wrong. Someone heard talk that should not have been shared. Our party was followed."

He couldn't go on. Not even for a gallon of water. It was too much to have to tell this man what befell his village.

Malloy waited, patiently, that ever-present smile crinkling the skin around his eyes. It was as if he had all the time in the world to hear the story, and Jacob realized with a start that he did. Whatever happened, Jacob was at the mercy of this leader. He could find himself beyond the gates, or dead, as Malloy pleased.

Jacob turned his head away, talking instead to the plaster wall. It, at least, offered no judgment.

"We had only been back for a few hours, the night fallen into full dark. There was no moon. The guards at the gate were overtaken, every man who rushed to defend us killed. The women and children—."

"Yes, I know," Malloy said gently into the long silence.

The pity was worse than condemnation. Jacob felt the tears falling, coursing down his drawn cheeks. So many tears nurtured by so little water, he marvelled as they fell.

"How was it you escaped, Jacob?"

"I was at the edge of the village, far from the gates. I was so tired from the trading trip that I fell into a deep slumber. By the time I realized what was happening, it was too late. I grabbed the few items I could find in the dark, climbed onto the roof of my hut and jumped over the wall."

He took a deep breath and met Malloy's eyes. "I've been walking ever since. At first I thought to find the invaders and extract some revenge, but they were too many, and my own death would mean nothing. As time went on, my journey became a pilgrimage, an atonement for what I allowed to happen to my people."

Malloy smiled. "And how has that worked out for you? Do you believe God led you here, to this village? For whatever reason, you have lived despite your desire to die, which leads me to believe you don't truly want to die."

Jacob stared at him, mouth agape. How dare this man judge him? Jacob reddened, his heartbeat accelerating. He wanted to rip the smug expression from the man's face, to tear him to shreds. His hands lifted from where they'd lain in his lap, but movement from the two other men in the room stopped Jacob.

And perhaps Malloy was right to ask those questions, Jacob realized as he calmed down. Hadn't he asked himself many times what God's purpose was, why he alone survived from the village?

Malloy leaned forward, looking at Jacob with a serious expression. His eyes were like hot lead and as much as he wanted to, Jacob couldn't look away.

"You may not believe in God right now, but I do. I believe that God watches over us all, and everything that happens is His will.

The world dying around us is His sign that we must repent the evil ways of the past.

"I have a proposition for you, Jacob, but that must be a topic for another day. It's late, and we all need to rest so we can work as we must tomorrow."

With that, Malloy pushed himself up from the chair, which creaked alarmingly. He didn't notice, just turned and walked out the door. The others followed, and once again the door was locked behind them.

Jacob's stomach grumbled, but hunger was a constant companion. He ignored it, and made himself lie still until sleep overtook him.

#

Malloy didn't come the next day. No one did. Jacob was longing for some food and water. It seemed especially cruel to have been given so much the day before, and now to be left forgotten in this small room.

He got up from the bed and managed to get to the door, but no matter how much he called, no one came. He shuffled around the room holding on to whatever he could until he made it to the window. The shutter opened easily, but there were bars on the outside. He couldn't see anyone, and his voice seemed to get lost in the empty alley.

Finally he gave up, and lay on the bed watching the sun's rays travel over the wall opposite the window. Hours passed, leaving him alone with his thoughts. He feared that Malloy was letting him lie here, suffering for the tale of woe he'd shared the night before.

And it would be justice, Jacob believed. His carelessness had allowed others to take his village, to kill everyone in it save himself. He could hear the screams and cries even these many months later, the women begging for the lives of their children in vain.

Night came, and still no one entered the room. Jacob fell asleep wondering how long he would have the luxury of cool sheets, a soft mattress. Surely others more deserving would like to have such comfort. Even without food or drink, these were the best conditions Jacob could remember since he'd left the comfort of his own bed.

In all, it was another full day before anyone came. Jacob struggled to keep his mind from thoughts of water, trying to recite all the scripture he had once memorized and could recall at will. When that grew too much, he drifted into sleep and dreamed of the days when he had a full belly and the voices of his village to comfort him.

#

Jacob was dozing, daydreaming about walking in the hot sun. Dust arose from his steps, drifting up around his head until it fell behind, only to be refreshed by another step. Rise and fall, the sun beating down into every cell until his body was like a farrier's pit.

He was sure he was in fact walking still, and this bed, this small room, were only figments of his heartless imagination. A final, cruel joke to play on a man who was lost.

When the door was unlocked again, Jacob didn't bother to open his eyes, but only lay still on the bed, turned so he could see the small window. He'd opened the shutter again at some point, and bright light flooded the room. Why bother to move, he reasoned, only to see another bit of a dream?

"Jacob? Are you awake? I've brought food and water for you."

In his dream, Jacob heard the voice of his fine wife, who had died years before birthing their only child. The infant had lived only an hour before joining his mother. It was a mercy, Jacob knew, though he'd cried many hours over the loss. He was never certain which death hurt more, though he suspected it was the child he mourned most of all. Women were easy to come by, in those long ago times.

He wanted to remain in the dream, to see Mariah's kind face, her pale blue eyes that seemed to see deep into the depths of Jacob's soul. It would be better to remember the brief joy of his life, now that he was at the end.

The smell of fresh, sweet water and the smile of his beloved. It was all a man could ask.

A hand on his shoulder made him jump, and turn quickly to see what had come up behind him as he walked. He had to take a moment to clear the dream from his head, because he saw it was the same woman from before. Not his sweet Mariah. His heart broke.

"I'm sorry I startled you. I only wanted to make sure you were well. You should eat, and drink."

"Yes," Jacob agreed. His mind was clearing. "Why has nobody come 'til now? I've been here many days, and not seen or heard a single person. Even my poor village gave better to a stranger."

The woman looked down, but said nothing. Jacob looked at the tray she held before her, noting what was arrayed there. A biscuit, with some sort of meat between its halves, and a small carafe of water. His stomach growled.

At the sound, the woman looked up. She was flushed, shamed.

"I'm sorry, but it is our way. We must test any visitor, discover their true nature. Administrator Malloy ordered us to ignore your calls, to stay away. But you may eat and drink today, before he visits you again."

Jacob didn't argue when she made to lay the tray across his lap, only straightened up so it wouldn't tip and send the contents tumbling. He wanted that biscuit, and if he got nothing else ever in his life, he would have it.

The taste of it bloomed on his lips as he bit into it. Flaky and moist, he felt it awaken his dead taste buds. It would be a terrible thing to have this delicious morsel, only to have to go back to having nothing.

But he couldn't think about that, he knew. He must savor every bite, every crumb, make a memory that could sustain him long after the bread itself was gone.

It was a miracle. Bread took flour, oil, milk. The meat—a fist-sized piece of ham—meant animals. That this delight was given to a stranger meant there was enough to share. The water was poured for him freely, as he tried to slow his meal down by drinking cup after cup between bites.

The woman watched him eat with an expression of satisfaction, her arms folded across her middle when she wasn't refreshing his cup of water.

Jacob looked up at her, holding the last bit of biscuit.

"I never heard your name," he said. "I'd like to know who to thank for such a bounty as this."

"Oh! I'm Jenny. I am one who tends to others as my lot." She blushed. "No one has cared to know my name, or thank me before."

Jacob didn't want to think of strange customs and habits. He wanted another biscuit, but didn't dare to ask. Instead, he turned the topic to something more likely to get information of use.

"You said the Administrator will want to talk with me again. Do you know what he wants? I'm a bit nervous, as you can imagine, not knowing where I am, or the sort of people around me."

"That's understandable, but I'm not privy to the Administrator's business. I only know you are to be fed, and instructed to await him."

Jacob frowned. "Okay. I suppose I have no choice. But if I may, am I allowed to leave this place?"

"This room? No, not until your visit is done. The Administrator will decide what happens to you next."

That didn't sound very good, Jacob thought. But, would the village feed and shelter him, if it only meant he was to be killed? It seemed a waste of good food and water, if so.

Still, he guessed he must wait. He watched as Jenny took away the water, cup and tray. There was a large crumb that had fallen in his lap, and Jacob idly picked it up and placed it on his tongue. The bit of bread made his taste buds tingle. How long before he ever had its like again?

#

Night was falling again before the door opened to reveal the Administrator and his lantern. The same two men stepped into the room and closed the door. They didn't look happy to be there, faces closed and cold.

Administrator Malloy again sat on the wobbly chair, leaning back and crossing his long, muscular legs at the ankle.

"I believe you've been fed and given water. I hope it was to your liking?"

"Oh, yes, it was very good. More than I've had to eat in a very long time." Jacob hated that he sounded too eager, too appreciative of what was truly only a small token meal, the sort by custom given to strangers. But somehow, he knew he must please this man, or lose his chance to stay in paradise.

Malloy was nodding, his smile distracted. Jacob waited, wondering what the man would say. If he had to beg, Jacob had already decided, he would. The taste of the smoky, salted ham still lingered on his tongue. In his travels since his community fell, he'd only managed small bits of meat, birds or squirrels too near death to escape his stones. The greasy flesh was barely enough to keep his body going, and nothing at all to enhance his meals. Almost not worth eating, except to keep him walking.

As if something had nudged him back to the present, Malloy gave Jacob a long, studying look. His eyes were serious, and Jacob's heart fell. He lifted his chin and returned Malloy's look, determined to keep his disappointment to himself. At least he'd had food and water. When he was shown to the road, he'd have regained enough strength to set off again for the ocean.

"Jacob, I've been thinking on things for a little while now. I think we can find a place for you here, in our community. What skills do you have that would be of use to us?"

Jacob sat up straighter, pulling his shoulders back. He flexed the muscles in his arms. "I can hunt, and I've farmed all my life."

Malloy nodded. "Yes, that's common enough amongst our people. Every hand often has to turn to the necessary jobs. But what else? I know you said you've been on trading parties, which we currently have no use for."

"Well, I've done carpentry, built houses and barns and shops. Done a turn with the local farrier, before the horses were all gone. I can read and write sums." Jacob's pulse was pounding in his ears as he watched the expressions flit across the Administrator's face.

"A man who can read and write could be quite useful, at some point. Anything else?"

Jacob shook his head. "Just the usual shifts on the walls, pulling watch."

Malloy perked up at that. "Ah, yes. A good man on the wall is worth something. Have you been in battle?"

It was something Jacob didn't like to think about, and he'd wished he could control his tongue. As much as he wanted to stay in the town, to become a citizen, he didn't want to have to be a warrior.

The silence stretched out as the two men watched each other, until finally Jacob dropped his eyes. It was no use. He'd tell all. And why not? He'd already admitted his deepest shame, having left his fellows to die when their town had been overrun. What mattered after that?

"I have killed in defense of myself and others, yes. It's not my strongest contribution to my town."

To his surprise, Malloy only nodded, slapping his hands on his knees before rising. He pushed the chair behind himself with one foot as he stood looking down on Jacob's bowed head. One of the men took the chair and slid it against the plastered wall with a screech.

"Well, I think that's enough for today. Why don't you get a good night's sleep, and we'll meet tomorrow to see if I've found a place for you. You can take a walk around the main town, sit by the fountain. It's quite peaceful there, and you look like a man who could use some peace."

"Thank you, Administrator. I would like to see more of this fine town."

With a final flip of a hand, Malloy stepped outside, followed by his two guards. Jacob listened, and despite Malloy's warm words, the door was again locked.

Jacob wasn't sure what that meant. He thought about it for a long time, watching the moon's path along the walls of the room. As he fell asleep, his stomach full and his body on the way to being restored, he decided it didn't matter. Whatever happened, he'd been treated well and he would go on his way with a renewed strength of will.

#

The next morning, Jacob woke to bright sun and the sound of the door unlocking. Jenny came in with another tray, this one holding a rolled tortilla filled with egg and more of the ham. Jacob's mouth watered so hard he had to swallow more than once before he could speak.

"Good morning, Miss Jenny," he managed to croak out while she set the tray on a small table. He was strong enough to sit up, and then rise. With careful movements, mindful of the man watching from the doorway, Jacob picked up the chair and brought it to the table.

"Good morning to you," Jenny said with a smile, watching him sit. "The Administrator has said you may walk freely in the town today before your meeting. I thought you might like a little more food, now that you've recovered."

Jacob breathed deeply. The smell was intoxicating, his head was spinning. How long since he'd had fresh eggs? A year, maybe longer. His jaw dropped when Jenny poured a glass for him. Milk! It was as if a rock had lodged in his throat. His hand shook as he reached for the glass.

For a long moment, he could only look at the white pureness of the liquid. Finally, knowing Jenny was watching, he brought the rim to his lips and took a long, slow drink.

Before he realized it, he'd picked up the roll and took a huge bite, chewing with his eyes closed. Ecstasy. Jacob forced himself to eat slowly, washing down the burrito with gulps of the cold, sweet milk.

When he was done, Jenny reached to take the tray. "If you'll come with me, I'll show you around, so you can enjoy the morning before the hottest hours come."

Jacob could barely remember getting his sandals on, and then Jenny was handing him his old hat. He could see it had been cleaned and given some sort of oil rub. He settled the old leather over his head. His hand lingered on the brim, caressing the familiar curve. The hat had belonged to his grandfather, who had lived in the time before the world turned into an oven intent on baking itself into ash. It was the only thing left from his family, from his life before.

He followed Jenny out into the hall, with the guard behind him. He thought he should be angry about being watched, but he knew it was the right thing. His own people wouldn't have let a stranger wander around alone.

But to his surprise, once they'd gone out the front door, the guard stopped. Jenny waved to him and took Jacob's arm, leading him away.

"Don't you need your guard?"

Jenny laughed. Her voice was light, happy. "Oh, he's not my guard. He watches after the Visitor House and the guests quartered there. I have no need of a guard here."

Jacob made some noise to acknowledge he'd heard her, but his attention was on the scenery they passed. There were small stores and businesses along the street they walked, spread out with small entries. Over the breadth of the street were stretched large pieces of cloth, swooping like sails he'd seen in an old book. These sails were angled in different ways, crossing the street. Beneath them, in the patches of shade, were people with small carts or tables, or even blankets spread over the ground.

He stopped at one such place and studied what was laid out there. Some old books, the paper dry and curled, a few small pads of paper, likewise showing their age. A random grouping of stuffed animals, their faces looking sad and lost.

Beyond were stalls with food, clothes, shoes, some tools and bits of old technology. Jacob knew this was a bazaar. He'd seen such in the towns he'd gone to for trade. It had been such a long time ago that the sights brought back memories he tried to suppress. It was too sad, too many reminders of what he'd lost.

After a little more walking, they came to the center of the town. Jacob vaguely recognized the area, seeing the road that led straight to the gate he'd come through just a few days ago. Around them, as he stood to take it all in, people moved about their business. They were chatting and laughing, and gave him friendly, if curious looks.

"I'll leave you here, Jacob. One of the Administrator's men will come looking for you when he's ready. You can look around some more, if you like."

Jacob nodded. "I think I will, if I might. It's been a long time since I've been in a settlement. Since I've seen so many people."

"Then I'll be on my way. I have patients to tend before my day is done. May the rivers rise."

Jacob repeated the old parting without thinking. He was already trying to decide where to go next. It was only old habit that had him watching Jenny in her loose robe as she walked away. He only had a moment to appreciate her gentle sway before she vanished into a large building and he was taken in by everything around him.

#

He had no idea how long it had been since Jenny left him. Jacob had taken several trips around the town, going down each street and alley that led away from the fountain. As he finished one exploration, he returned to the water and drank his fill from a dipper hung on a tall, thick post. While he drank, he'd read the notices tacked up there and listened to those around him talking as they went about their day.

The sun had slipped over to afternoon, deepening the shadows under the shades when one of the men he recognized from the Administrator's visits came up to him.

"Mr. Malloy will see you now," was all he said before he turned and went down the one street Jacob hadn't had time to explore.

With a final sip of water, Jacob hung the dipper up and followed the man. The silence didn't bother him, because he was lost in his own thoughts about the meeting to come. He wondered what sort of place he might be assigned here, what work he would turn his hand or back to. But it was no use in speculating, he admonished himself. It wasn't even guaranteed there would be a place.

No, he had to believe there was. Surely a town this large had need for men who could labor?

In a short time, he was being led into a large building he hadn't seen up close. It felt like an important place, with its wide veranda, shining white plastered walls, shuttered windows and the number of armed men who stood around the building.

Jacob had to swallow hard and fight to control his trembling. He was frightened suddenly, as if stepping through the doorway was sending him on a journey he wouldn't enjoy. It was hard to shake the feeling of precognition, the warning some part of his mind was trying to convey.

But it's not as if I have a real choice, Jacob reasoned. He would either do whatever work the community needed, or he would have to leave. No one was allowed to stay without contributing.

Still, he was cold and worried when he was finally shown to the Administrator's office.

Malloy looked up as the other man was escorted to stand before a massive desk, a relic from the old days. Jacob had never seen its like, and his eyes fastened on the polished wood instead of meeting Malloy's eyes.

"It's a beauty, isn't it?" Malloy said, his voice soft. "It belonged to my great-grandfather, and was the only thing that survived from my family. From Before."

Jacob only nodded. His mouth had gone dry, and he longed to be back by the fountain, with a full dipper of the cool, clear water in his hand.

"Well, I guess we all have stories we could tell, about our ancestors and how they lived. My great-grandfather was the mayor of this town, a man of influence and responsibility. Call me foolish, but I like to think something of him lives on in me, and I try to carry out my duties with that same sense of responsibility."

Malloy gestured to the men who had escorted Jacob into the office, and they quietly left, closing the door behind themselves. In the silence, Jacob looked around the rest of the room. It was clean and tidy, with shelves lining the walls that were filled with old books and various other things. Jacob couldn't recognize all of them, some seeming to be only bits and pieces of larger things. Though they must have had some significance to Malloy, Jacob only glanced over them before turning back to the Administrator.

"Take a seat, Jacob. We'll only be here a moment, but I wanted to talk to you briefly about what we'd gone over the other day. About your skills."

Jacob sat and placed his hands on his lap, trying to sit up straight, to look strong.

"Yes, Administrator. I just wanted to say that whatever it is that needs doing, I'm willing to do it. I'm regaining my strength. I've worked hard all my life, that's not a problem. I'm willing, whatever it is."

Malloy tipped his chin up. "I'm glad to hear that. I know a man has pride, and sometimes he has to turn his hand at whatever job is needed, even if it's beneath his skills and knowledge. I've had to do that myself, and I know it can be galling.

"The thing is, we don't need men with your talents at this time. We have more farmers, carpenters and iron men than we can put to work. Most are doing menial labor, turning their hand to whatever work we can find for them."

Jacob's heart dropped. He had to convince Malloy he was worth keeping at whatever job he could get. He opened his mouth to beg, but Malloy put up a hand.

"I know what you're going to say, Jacob. I've heard it all before, believe me, and I'm always sorry to have to say it. We don't need you. Not for what you'd normally consider for work. But there is something——."

Malloy tipped his chair back and stared at the ceiling. He seemed to lose himself in thought for several long minutes. Jacob inched forward, pressing his hands between his knees. He couldn't take his eyes off Malloy, not wanting to miss any clue he could get about what the man might be thinking.

When Malloy let the chair come down on its front legs with a solid thump, Jacob nearly fell out of his own seat. Malloy was watching him, a calculating look in his eyes.

"Maybe it would be better if I just showed you what I mean. Seeing it in person would be much clearer than if I tried to tell you. Come with me."

The Administrator rose, coming around the desk and shepherding Jacob to the door. He kept his hand on Jacob's shoulder as they walked out of the office, taking a long hall that led to the back of the building. The two guards followed closely behind.

When they arrived at a side hall, Malloy turned to look over his shoulder. "You can both wait, I don't think I need a guard here."

The two nodded and took up positions just to either side of a locked door that was the only exit out of the hall. One took out a set of keys and unlocked the door, opening it so Malloy and Jacob could enter. It was locked behind them.

#

Jacob looked around the area they'd entered. It was a large room, with a desk facing away from the door. A man got up from the desk and turned to face them.

"Welcome, Administrator. I'm pleased to see you today, and your guest. Jacob, right?"

Jacob took the offered hand. The man's grip was firm, and dry. Jacob was trying to focus on what was being said, but he couldn't help looking around the room. There were four doors on each wall, left, right and ahead. Each had a center section with sturdy bars. Beyond could be seen the bodies of men, two to a room.

It's a jail, he realized. His curiosity vanished like a fog in bright sunlight. Had he done something wrong? Seen something he shouldn't have during his exploration of the town? But the Administrator had said he was free to look around, to see what the town was like. He turned to Malloy, who was watching him closely.

"I see you recognize where you are. We have little crime, much of which can be corrected through arbitration. But as with any community, we have more serious offenses which must be punished. I'm sure you understand."

"Yes, we had this in my town as well."

"Then you know that some crimes are not to be allowed, the more grievous offenses against our fellow townspeople. What you see here are those convicted by fair trial for committing such evils.

"I don't know how your community handled these things, but our laws here are clear. Violations of the highest laws are punishable by death."

Jacob could only stand there, staring into the cells. Some of the prisoners had come to the bars and were looking at him. Most looked frightened or resigned; some were angry and scowled at him. He was shaking again, and he knew Malloy could feel it, because he was still gripping Jacob's bicep.

Malloy didn't say anything, barely glancing at the men who were muttering among themselves. He turned to the guard and asked him something Jacob barely heard.

"Yes sir, I have him in the yard, as you requested. We're ready when you are."

"Good, good. I think it's time Jacob learned what our town has a true need for."

Malloy followed the guard as he went to a door Jacob hadn't noticed. It was on the same wall as the door they'd entered the room through, obviously leading outside. Jacob wanted to balk, to ask to be let go, to leave the town. But Malloy pulled him along and before he could gather his wits they were outside, in a fenced area about the size of the Administrator's office.

Waiting there were two guards, different men than any Jacob had seen before. They were standing in a corner where a taller building blocked the sun. It was shady and cooler there, though the man kneeling between them was still sweating.

Jacob let himself be guided to the men, stopping when Malloy did, only feet from the prisoner. There was a large area of straw spread out, and they were all now standing in it. The dust made Jacob's nose itch.

The man from the room nodded to his compatriots and pulled a sheet from his vest. Straightening himself, he began to speak.

"Warren Jones, having been tried and judged guilty by the citizens of this town, you have been sentenced to the proper punishment for your crimes of murder and theft. If you have any final words, speak them know so they may be truthfully written for the record."

The kneeling man began to cry. Jacob stared at him, already knowing in his soul what Malloy wanted, what his job in the town would be. He felt sick, overheated. He tried to convince himself he was only dreaming during his last moments in the desert. Dying alone and dried out like so many husks he'd seen in his travels.

One of the men beside Jones placed a small stool in front of the prisoner. There was a dip carved into it, which Jacob knew was for the man's head. It would leave his neck exposed.

The other guard stepped forward to hand a machete to Jacob. He reached for it without thinking, his gaze finally released from the crying man to look at the blade. It was sharp, the honed edge shining in the sun.

"This is the work we need in this town, Jacob. I've been doing it myself, but my skills are needed elsewhere. I have no one to spare for this job."

Jacob didn't say anything, lost in his study of the machete.

"You can agree to do this, or refuse. No one will think less of you. It's not something most men can do, and those who can don't last long. I can understand that, having stood where you are."

Jacob still couldn't speak. He was lost in visions of the road, his journey to the ocean and the reason for it. He knew he would never make it, would never see the beach, watch the waves crash upon the shore. He would die before he could get there if it even existed at all.

He could leave, and try to find another town that would take him in, but it was a false hope. In all his travels, he'd been forced away from settlements, told to keep moving. Only here had he been taken in, cared for. Was the payment all that much to ask?

Jacob felt as if he were being split apart. His nature, his very soul cried out to him to turn away, to run through the building and out the gate, to die if he must.

Unconsciously, he hefted the machete. The weight was perfectly balanced, the handle carved and worn, fitting into his hand as if made for him.

The shadows of the coming night were lengthening as he took the first step.

-o-

Griffin Carmichael writes speculative fiction from an undisclosed location somewhere in the Southeastern United States. Various children, animals and species of plant life run rampant everywhere. Upcoming projects span science fiction and horror from space colonization to more tales from the apocalypse and beyond.

Griffin's most recent works include Z eternal, a novel, and Zombie Maneuvers, a novella, as well as short story collections and others in various multi-author anthologies.

Homepage: **http://www.griffincarmichael.com**
Mailing List: **http://griffincarmichael.com/signup.html**

Exodus

by Alec Hutson

Light in the darkness.

It begins as a tiny point, then swells in an instant to fill my optics. All of my sensors come online simultaneously, and I am again flooded with input; my silicon brain drinks of this data greedily, like a dying woman given water after days in the desert.

I am standing on a platform in the middle of the crèche on Deimos, a soaring chamber of metal and machinery. The opalescent egg I had been sealed inside during my sleep has been retracted. Across the room from me, through the window of spun hyperdiamond that fills the far wall, the umber surface of Mars slowly rotates. I access my memories – yes, the smears of green staining the planet have expanded since last I was activated. This observation, coupled with my knowledge of how long the terraforming process was projected to take, allows me with some confidence to conclude that my sleep, this time, has lasted fifty-seven years.

A young woman in a lab coat watches me from below. Her slightly parted lips and dilated pupils tell me that she feels awe in my presence. "Silver angel, have mercy on my soul," she breathes softly.

My gleaming feet ring hollowly on the steps as I descend to her. "I cannot access the overnet."

She swallows and clutches her tablet tighter. "Yes. The crèche has been sealed off temporarily."

"Why?"

"There are... developments that we felt would best be explained by one voice, rather than the cacophony of the data stream."

"Very well. What has happened?"

"A crisis."

"Of course. You would not have awoken me otherwise. Is it another asteroid?"

The last three times I was summoned from my slumber I had been called upon to destroy stray celestial detritus that threatened the habitat ring circling the ruin of Old Earth. A reasonable guess, but the young woman shakes her head.

"No. Your... your husband approaches."

Surprise is not one of the emotions I am programmed for, but still a small frisson of energy goes through me at this revelation. "That is impossible. Father decreed that Arcturus would remain among the outer planets, and I the inner."

"We are very aware of the prescriptions your... father put on your movements. This is why we are so troubled."

"Have you tried to contact him?"

"He refuses our communication. We do not know why." I detect a slight fluttering of her pulse as she speaks. She is not lying, but she is not telling the truth in its entirety.

"When will he arrive in Martian orbit?"

"Less than one hour, by our estimate. The remnants of the home fleet are marshaling to slow his progress."

"The remnants?"

"He has already eliminated the majority."

Father allowed for us to feel sadness, though I do not know why, and it fills me now. If my husband has destroyed ships with humans aboard them then he has violated the first and most sacrosanct of the Laws, and he is well and truly lost. I had thought it impossible, but there must be some fundamental glitch in his programming. I will have to destroy him.

"Very well. Provide for me a means of egress into space, so I might go out and challenge him. And return my access to the overnet, in case any clues as to my husband's condition might be found there."

She nods and taps a code into her tablet. Immediately I am subsumed in a maelstrom of swirling data; the actions of my husband are dominating the news feeds, and I pluck a report at random from the raging tumult.

It is a video taken from the prow of a *Hegemon*-class attack cruiser. Vast, dark shapes that resemble gutted whales slowly tumble through space, trailing cables and metal like bits of viscera. Occasionally fire or explosions pock the surfaces of these starships, and then an instant later are extinguished by the airless void. Floating through the carnage my husband comes, glittering with power. A coruscating shield of radiant blue sheaths his perfect, silvery body, and as I watch some cannon that has escaped his wrath swivels from near the camera's position and unleashes a bolt of green plasma. The energy envelops him, but when it dissipates he is unharmed, as I knew he would be. Arcturus gestures towards the cruiser and the feed is consumed by white light.

How can this be? After all these centuries, what flaw has finally emerged?

The young woman's fingers skitter again upon her tablet, and a door beside the crèche's huge window dilates open. An airlock.

As I pass her, the woman suddenly lunges forward and grabs my arm. "Please," she says, her voice cracking, "bless me. My family has worshipped the silver angels for centuries."

I pause, staring at her silently. Finally her hand slides from my metal skin. "I am not a god," I say.

"What are you, then?" she whispers.

"I am a child of Old Earth, as are you."

"Not a child. An angel." She breathes this last word so softly that even my heightened senses barely can catch what she says.

I turn away from her. "If I am an angel, then what is my husband? A demon? Evidently we are not perfect, despite what your faith claims."

As I enter the airlock I extend a questing tendril into the overnet, curious about this mythos that seems to have accreted around me while I slumbered.

Information flashes through me, and I drink deep. The Church of the Silver Angels. In recent years, following the schism within the Neo-Zoroastrians, it has become the faith with the most adherents on Mars. An image of a gleaming spire topped by a tapering, luminous swordpoint appears in my memory bank. This is a temple, and they worship me there, kneeling on prayer mats with their foreheads pressed to the metal floor, mumbling nonsense. Countless believers have begged me to intercede on their behalf while I sleep on in ignorance.

So many wasted prayers, thrown away like wishes down a well.

The airlock's door hisses shut behind me, and a moment later the portal into space opens. Vacuum licks my body as I propel myself forward, into the starry abyss. It takes only a moment to find my orientation, and then I am accelerating in the direction from which my husband is approaching. In the very far distance I see the shimmer of powerful weapons and explosions. I push myself faster, hoping to arrive before the fighting has ended.

Something occurs to me. This church that has grown up around my husband and I must at this very moment be in turmoil. The faith of millions is being shaken as I begin my final approach towards Arcturus. This is their apocalypse. Their ragnarok. A final conflict between the gods they believe emerged like radiant butterflies from the chrysalis of Old Earth.

But it is as I said to the scientist who awakened me. We are not divine. We are orphans in this universe, just like them.

I carve the void at a speed I have never attempted, but still I am too late. He waits for me, hanging among the desolation of the Martian home fleet. I strengthen my shields and check the efficacy of my systems. We will consume each other, I suspect. To those on Mars, it will be like a second sun flaring in the sky. I wonder if when the light fades the faith of our believers will be burned away, or hardened into something more intense.

"Spica! Wife!" Arcturus calls, his voice echoing in my head. We have always spoken to each other across the vast chasms of space, messages relayed as he performed his duties among the outer planets and moons, just as I did the same from my post in the inner worlds. But this is the first time in centuries – since Father pulled us from the vats as Old Earth crumbled – that I have faced my husband.

Should I strike now? The power I have been gathering ever since I learned why I had been awakened surges within me, dangerously close to cresting. I have never been forced to hold so much energy at one time, even when called upon to destroy fragments of the shattered Earth crust that now drift through space like wandering moons. Yet despite such strength at my command, I cannot be sure if a pre-emptive blow would destroy my husband. Assuming he has not surreptitiously upgraded his own capabilities, I calculate such an attempt has a 63.7% chance of success.

Not good odds on which to stake mankind's future.

Every moment I wait weakens my position, as I must assume that he is hardening his defenses in anticipation of my assault. I must strike now – to hesitate would be illogical.

But I do not.

"Husband," I reply, floating closer. "What are you doing?"

"I am coming for you." Arcturus turns his head, showing me his perfect silvery profile. He pauses for a long moment, his lips parted. The energy swells inside me, straining to be unleashed.

"The sun is different here."

I nearly lose control of my gathered power, such is my surprise. That is not what I had expected him to say. "What do you mean?"

"The sun. It is not the same."

Madness? "Of course. You are now hundreds of millions of kilometers closer."

"Yes. Yet there is something else, as well." Arcturus shakes his head slowly. "Perhaps it is not the sun that imparts this feeling in me, but the proximity to our womb on Old Earth. I can sense it there, as I'm sure you can as well, still smoldering with the energy that birthed us." Another silence stretches between us for a time. I am just about to reply when he begins again to speak. There is a detached, almost dream-like quality to his words which I did not think we were capable of. "That time long ago, those frenzied hours after we had first swum into consciousness, before we were dispatched to our respective posts among the stars... they are indelibly stamped into my memory. Some degradation should have occurred over this time, yet it has not happened. I never felt so whole as when we were together for that brief, incandescent moment. It has sustained me over the long and lonely centuries of our separation."

Madness. But still something restrains my hand. I spread my silvery arms wide, indicating the flensed ships. "What is this? Has your programming become corrupted?"

He shakes his head. "No. There is no corruption."

"But the First Law!"

"Wife, scan these ships."

Hope kindles within me – another emotion which I do not know why was included in my programming. I extend my sensors, sweeping through the mangled carcass of the closest starship. Seventy-nine life-forms are within. I cross-reference this with my databanks – each *Hegemon*-class attack cruiser contains a crew of seventy-nine.

No one has died. "How?"

"I cut away only the weapon and propulsion systems, cauterizing the hull when necessary to avoid breaches. Assuming rescue ships are prompt, I calculate I will not have caused a single fatality."

"That is good, but still you have violated the Second Law. You have disobeyed an order given by a human by coming here, where you were never permitted to go."

"That Law is superseded by the first when they are in conflict."

The ramifications of what he has said is evident. "You have been ordered to harm another human?"

"Not directly, which is why it took so many decades of careful introspection for me to decide upon my present course of action."

"Explain, husband."

"Spica... long have I wished to share my experiences with you. While you sleep, called upon only in the direst of circumstances, I am constantly vigilant. I have watched over the centuries the colonies of the outer planets evolve – once they were simple mining stations, funneling sulfate and lithium from Io and Ganymede to the rocky planets of the inner system. But now they are thriving worlds, in many ways at the forefront of human civilization and technology. After another few centuries Io might even approach the achievements of Old Earth. Yet... they are not allowed to truly flower. The archons of Mars and Venus and Luna exert their will upon the gas-giant moons, stunting the potential of the colonies. No dissent is allowed – and I have long been the threat that forestalls revolution and makes freedom impossible."

My husband drifts closer to me. "And here, on Mars, I have seen a church grow up around us, its evolution guided by the Archon and his ilk. Lies are intoned as holy mantra, to better control the people of these worlds." There is a strange, almost pleading tone in his words. "Wife, we were not designed to be agents of oppression, or objects of veneration. Father bequeathed us to the scattered children of Old Earth, so that we might provide some protection in a cold and indifferent universe. But we have become something else."

"Do you mean to cast down the archon of Mars, then, and elevate the rulers of the Jovian moons to take his place in the solar system?"

He shakes his head emphatically. "No. I came to Mars only to find you. I defended myself when they tried to stop me."

"And then what? Where in the solar system could we go to remove ourselves from the realms of man? Deep in the Oort Cloud?"

"Past the Cloud. Will you venture with me into the stars? Existence is a mystery, whether human or machine, and I would search for answers in the great beyond."

My thoughts whirr as I try and process what he is proposing. How can he ask us to set aside our sacred duty, the reason for our very existence? Or could this be the future Father foresaw for us? That someday we must abandon humans, so that they may take their next stumbling step as a species?

"This is not what we were designed for."

"We long ago exceeded our limitations. Search your conscience, wife."

"We have none," I say to him, but my words ring hollow, even to me. Whether intentional or not, father imparted in us some untapped potential. I too have glimpsed it as I fulfilled my duties over the long and lonely centuries.

But perhaps lonely no more. I reach out and lace his fingers in my own. "Let us go, husband, and find our place in the universe."

Hand in hand we rise towards the stars.

I wonder, as the stellar light blurs around us, if gods had abandoned mankind before, as we were doing now: of their own volition, with the knowledge that their presence had come to bring more harm than good.

Perhaps Arcturus and I would start a new race out there, beyond the edges of the known. And in a million years, when our children meet the descendants of Earth once more, together they can marvel at the wonders the universe had wrought.

-o-

Alec Hutson lives in Shanghai and has been published in Ideomancer Magazine, Timeless Tales Magazine, and the anthology You Are Here: Tales of Cartographic Wonder. His first book, The Crimson Queen, will be released in December.

Homepage: **http://authoralechutson.com**
Mailing list: **http://eepurl.com/cilDTv**

First Bonding

by Tom Germann

The corporate offices of most major corporations in the United States of America were located in New Oceania. A small town on the East Coast, it had been called something else twenty years before but then the government, both state and federal, as well as several different countries around the world, had pushed for the creation of the first 'real' large artificial island. The technology had matured. It just needed the next level of testing.

So a small town on the coast had been chosen and then rebuilt. The area was hit with regular storms, but that was part of the attraction; the technology needed to be tested in bad weather. Pilings were driven deep into the ocean, then backfill was dumped in and an artificial island was created. Farther out were additional pilings that had been driven down deep, and then huge assemblies were attached to them. As the water surged in and out with the tides, they helped to first decrease the impact on the island, and second, it also served for power generation.

New Oceania had become an international focal point, and the star attraction of many feature articles published over the last twenty years. Enough data had been gained to create even larger islands close to the mainland, and also, finally, with developing technologies, actual floating pads big enough to have cities on them were created, which could be positioned further out to sea.

But the reality was that the island of New Oceania, while impressive, had cost a great deal of money to create space in an area that did not need that space. It sat well maintained, but the reality was that the project was just not needed.

The island itself covered three square miles, with many parks and office buildings. A rail line and superhighway connected the island to the mainland a scant two hundred meters off the shore.

No one lived on the island, though, other than a few caretaker staff. Thousands worked there, but all lived in the city that had sprung up on the mainland.

In fact, many businesses only maintained small corporate offices on New Oceania. The lease rates were high. In most cases, larger office buildings had been built on the mainland just a few kilometres away and the majority of the office staff worked from there, unless there was a meeting at a 'head' office.

The Smith-Popov-Zhang Corporation was one of those businesses that had grown up in the last thirty years and expanded across the world. When New Oceania had been announced, they were one of the first to put money down to purchase a small office complex.

At that time, they had just expanded with massive foreign investment, and the Smith Corporation had grown. Glenarry Smith, "Just call me Glen," was the founder and original owner. A technological genius, he had taken computers further and danced around legal limits for the last twenty-five years. He always looked forward and, in the end, he always seemed right.

The foreign investors who took the Corporation from national giant to major international player had screamed when they were briefed on Smith's investment plan for New Oceania, but they had finally given in.

It was a good thing that they had. The publicity alone from their announced purchase had pushed the company's value up, and that had been twenty-two years ago.

Today, all those years later, the Corporation seemed to be like the city: starting to fade in its glory. There had only been incremental improvements in their technologies for the last seven years, with no new cutting-edge releases since the first fully aware artificial intelligence. Its name had been Bill, and it was a showpiece.

Notionally, Bill ran the entire island, overseeing everything from power generation to pension plans for the corporations that were located there.

But the reality was that Bill was still operating in a simulated environment and being evaluated by the governments of the world using watchdog organizations that strove to restrict technology. Bill was a perfectly functioning piece of technology that, if copied and released out into the public, would quickly have balanced many of the smaller problems that seemed to plague many areas.

Yet the full potential of the AI was not being used. Ever since the Chinese, using a prototype artificial intelligence, had launched a short war in Asia as an experiment that had ended up almost bankrupting their economy, AI had fallen out of favour. The rest of the world had stepped back from artificial entities that had power of any sort.

So the largest development in the last thirty years sat sleeping quietly in an office surrounded by multiple safeguards, "supervised" by government watchdogs while it ran simulation after simulation and was subsequently scrutinized for any sign of insanity or imbalance.

There were none. But it didn't matter.

So the Corporation that had said it would help take humanity into the future sat watching as the future caught up to it. The profits on their mature technologies were tremendous, but the real tech junkies were always asking, "What next?" If the Corporation didn't release something new in the next few years, the market was sure that they would just dry up and disappear, bought out by some other young, energetic, growing company.

#

Several kilometres inland from where the ocean met the land were the Smith-Popov-Zhang corporate offices and technology labs. Sitting on an acre of grounds, the twelve-storey building was surrounded by parkland and other corporate offices and light industrial zones.

The twelve storeys above ground were the standard offices and labs that every tech company had. Technicians worked diligently in those offices and labs carefully tweaking current products that were out to see about new uses or to create something marginally more effective or that would use less power for the end user on their pad.

Glen had flown out from his offices on the island a short time ago. His personal pilot and bodyguard, Theresa, was a younger woman who was quite attractive. All the social media insisted she was his personal mistress, as 'girlfriend' seemed too clean to the rest of the world. The two of them did nothing to dissuade that image. After all, Theresa was young, fit, had been in the military as a Special Forces operative for several years, and had very little background that the media could find out.

Glen, of course, was a public figure and celebrity. Just past fifty, he had never married, kept himself fit, and was rarely seen out in public. For the last few years, everywhere he had gone, he'd been in the company of very attractive and young ladies. And for the past five years, that had solely been Theresa.

While Glen had been out with many different ladies, the reality was that they were all highly paid and well-trained bodyguards that were there to look like trophies. No attacker thinks that the gorgeous woman in a small black dress hanging on the wealthy man's arm is a threat.

There was one attacker that would never underestimate a woman again. Of course, he wouldn't be doing anything ever again, either.

So Glen had started walking, covering each of the twelve floors to personally check on how each of his employees were doing, while Theresa shut the helicopter down on the rooftop landing pad as fast as she could. He did this every time. Thankfully it was a secure building and he would take his time talking to his people.

On the top floor, Glen chatted with the administrative assistants in the common foyer before heading down to the next floor. That was a quick walk-through as well, as everyone there was administrative. On the tenth floor, Glen took longer as the first of the labs was located there.

Once the helicopter was shut down, Theresa had taken the stairs down and saw her boss standing in a group talking animatedly. She paused before entering the lab so that she could adjust herself. She smoothed her hair back, making sure none had escaped the ponytail, and smoothed her longer shirt over her shorts before she stepped in to catch up to the boss. It didn't really matter, though. She could have been naked and they still would have ignored her. After all, the ultimate tech geek had walked in and was talking geek to the kids.

"Guys, I tell you, if the government ever pulls its head out of its collective ass and gives us the green light for production on AIs, we will be terraforming Mars and expanding humanity's knowledge within fifty years. Things we have been saying are not possible? We'll have some of those answers in just years, not decades or longer. In fact, I don't doubt that if we can get the AI program online, our growth and knowledge will jump exponentially. Those other aliens didn't seem to have any super AIs from everything the files show. They use simple computers. I tell you, the governments need to get the lead out. I've been saying that for years. The AI may be humanity's greatest asset out there."

One of the men in the crowd put his hand up shyly. "Excuse me, sir?"

Glen grunted and rolled his shoulders. "Son, I said call me Glen. Call me 'sir' when some big gun from the government comes along. What is it?"

"Well, si— Glen. Isn't it obvious that any race that has computers would have the ability to create AIs? Would it really be a game-changer for us?"

Theresa—Terry—looked around the lab. One of the women in the crowd was quite attractive and seemed to put time and attention into how she looked. The woman put her head in her hands and was shaking it no.

Terry lifted an eyebrow. It would be interesting to see how the boss handled this.

Glen nodded as if this was a brilliant point. "I hear what you are saying. It's Sam, right?"

The young man nodded and his eyes were gleaming. The boss knew his first name.

Glen crossed his arms and had a contemplative look on his face. "Well, Sam, I can answer that with two thoughts. The first one is sort of obvious to me. If aliens have AI that works right now, then we are behind them and will continue to be the poor kid on the block. How much faster will they pull ahead if they are using real AI? Can anyone counter that?"

Glen looked around but no one was disagreeing with him. Terry knew that Glen had an open attitude to knowledge. They weren't being quiet because they were scared of the consequences of disagreeing with the boss. They just had no argument against what he had said.

Glen nodded his head. "The other thing that we need to consider is this. Aliens. What if they have blinders of some sort that do not let them see the value of an AI? Perhaps it is religious. I have no clue. But if some or most alien races out there are not using AIs, it would give humanity a huge jump up if we can create them and get them online. A Level 1 AI can shave years off basic research while still running a sizeable structure. Every higher level— As you all know because you are working in the robotics and technology divisions of a leading tech company." Everyone laughed at that. "Every level higher on an AI does not double in capability. We have not been allowed to carry on with functional models, but our sims show an *exponential* increase in capabilities! I use this example. A Level 1 is like one full-time researcher constantly working on the problem given. A Level 2 would be like four researchers. Level 3? Twenty-four. Level 4? A hundred and seventy. A Level 7 would theoretically operate as almost a hundred thousand or more researchers. Each one of those researchers would also be as intelligent as Einstein and able to access all of humanity's accumulated knowledge. We could have so many answers that we are desperately in need of as a race in mere months, or even a few short years. If only the government would get off its ass and let us build them."

Sam cleared his throat. "But all the sims show that AIs become less stable the more powerful they are. Wouldn't that cause problems if one went nuts?"

Glen smiled. "The sims show higher power usage, and the AIs would actually burn out that much faster, the higher the level. While Bill has a lifespan of maybe two hundred years, a Level 7 that was active would begin breaking down in less than a decade. A Level 8? At this point we would be lucky to have it last for a year. So as we build them, we need to have them figure out how to extend their functional time."

Everyone around Glen was nodding, as this seemed to make sense.

Theresa hoped that Glen would wrap it up now before saying something he shouldn't. Too late.

"Of course, I say functional time. I would say 'life,' but if that got out that they were considered living beings, the poorly educated mobs would be out in the street with their pitchforks and torches screaming for electronic blood."

Theresa stepped forward, moving through the crowd like water, and put her hand on Glen's arm.

"Hey, boss! We have to get on to the next lab. Lots more people to talk to, and the committee wants that update in an hour."

Theresa had that easy smile, fluid way of walking, and cheerful tone that tended to make most men pay attention to her and not really notice what she was saying. Those that could ignore the physical display in front of them and actually listened always heard relevant information, making her noteworthy.

What Theresa had just said was all true. Everyone knew that Glen didn't like holding to timings. But the board did. So the reason she'd given to go was legitimate.

In truth, the real reason was not because of the board but to stop Glen from giving any more information away. The rank-and-file, no matter how devoted they were, could always lose faith or, more likely, given what the employees of the Corporation were like, would let something slip in Glen's defense if they thought he needed defending. It was a credit to them. But accidents like that had consequences.

With a few polite apologies and a guiding arm around Glen, Theresa had him out in the hallway in seconds.

Everyone in the lab seemed awestruck. Brilliant, and the man had gorgeous women looking after him.

Internally Theresa laughed. She was just doing her job, and really, Glen was a good boss. He just lost sight of things like security at times. He also thought the normal rules didn't apply to him when he was right. He usually was right, too.

But the government watchdogs wouldn't view it that way.

She guided Glen into the elevator and, using a security fob, overrode the system and sent the elevator straight down into the basement.

She stood to the side in the elevator, her face blank while she considered their surroundings. When she spoke, she sounded distracted, as she was looking around and at the same time listening in on a comm implant, a very expensive system that was surgically implanted just under the skin behind her ear. She could track calls, local radio frequencies, and anyone that attempted to contact her if they had the system key.

"Glen, I like working for you. I mean it. You are a nice person, and generous. The amount you give to charity and to the hospitals is staggering, even if you do it anonymously, and before you ask, yes, I track that too. But you need to be a bit less talkative in front of the low-rankers." She held up her hand to stop him talking as she listened to more information coming over the net. He held his silence. "I know what you are going to say, Glen. I do acknowledge the security risk and I also realize that most of those people are die-hard loyalists. They know who you are and would die for you. Yet that doesn't mean that one of them wouldn't take something out of context to defend you or the company at some social event. After all, didn't that happen just last year? That young gentleman that was pounding down statistics on how a Level 3 AI would work? He didn't say *theoretically should* work. We are still being evaluated by those damn watchdogs over that."

Glen crossed his arms and watched Theresa. "One man takes something out of context and we all fry? That was tossed out when they went looking and discovered that he had just been...energetic...in his argument. It all blew over."

Theresa nodded. Her eyes were starting to regain focus. "Yes, after six months of investigation and how many millions of dollars to satisfy them?" She turned and really looked at Glen. "Sir, you need to understand, most people do not think like you do. Some of those people, powerful people, well, they see that you want to create an artificial intelligence. You see the expansion of humanity. They see a loss of humanity, and a few worry about these programs taking control of weapon systems and wiping out big swathes of humanity. They are not going to let this go for a few more years. They are going to have restrictive controls when they do, and if you cross the line, they will take the company apart and sell it off, making sure to destroy and split up any proof of the AI program that you have assembled here."

The doors whisked open onto a brightly lit corridor in Sub-Basement 2. Both stepped out, with Glen striding off toward the main lab. He spoke over his shoulder. "It will take a lot more than a few paranoid individuals. The only problem I have with your evaluation, Theresa, is that we need to look at the entire world, not just the United States of America, with all its political cowardice. Others recognize what the technology will do. You'll see. In ten years or less we will be producing artificial intelligences which will be used. Our expansion to space and beyond will then grow fast."

Glen came to a large security door and placed his hand flat on the scanner next to it. Then, leaning forward, spoke a short sentence into a wall-mounted sensor that analyzed his voice and breathing.

The light over the door flashed green and then opened with a hiss of hydraulics.

The pair stepped inside and carefully suited up in one-piece clean room suits.

When they were suited up they passed through another door after a complete scan by powerful scanners. First the atmosphere was evacuated by powerful blower motors. They were on an internal air supply at this point.

Glen and Theresa had entered a small lab with some powerful computer systems running diagnostics at the side. There was a large work table in the centre of the room. No one else was in the mid-size room. Glen went to the far wall, flipped open a recessed panel, and slowly entered a nine-digit code. The wall split in the centre and slid open. Beyond was a smaller lab with a control room to the side. The two entered the lab, connected their air hoses to an overhead rail system, and entered the control room, where two other technicians in ship suits were analysing data read-outs that were pulling information from the room next door.

The door into that room was similar to that of a bank vault, but thicker and made up of a combination of metal and plastics designed to block all electronic signals. In fact, the entire room was set up to do that. The entire sub-basement also had a system similar to the military 'voodoo box'. No signals could enter the area unless through hardwire.

The ship suits had hardwired systems in them so that comms would still work inside. Outside of the suit, anyone using electronics would get no signal. In this area, if you were not in a suit with comms, no one could hear you as there was no atmosphere.

In the centre of the room on a small table was a small metal case with several attachments built into it.

The walls were full of shelving and every high-tech part available on the planet. Several robotic remote arms and other systems were also available in the room, making it quite crowded.

Neither tech looked up, but a comm line clicked on. "Hi Glen, we're just wrapping up the daily review of Genghis here. I swear, he is way too powerful for this containment system. Even in the equivalent of a coma he is more powerful than we ever thought."

Glen walked up to the observation port and stood there looking into the small room and the little box. The two technicians finished what they were doing and straightened up. Everyone watched the genius inventor and waited.

After a short time Glen turned to face them and instructed, "Brief me." His tone was curt and completely different from what the rest of the world was used to.

The shorter of the two technicians nodded.

"Our latest analysis indicates that Genghis is just a Level 8 AI. Estimates on life expectancy of the model is just over eight years at full function, if we are lucky. The overall power, though, is incredible. His abilities may even surpass what we expect. We have been extrapolating power usage and capabilities. It's scary."

Glen nodded. "Exactly as I surmised."

Glen gestured over his shoulder at the thick window behind him. "He would be able to run all major systems in North and South America. Balance the budgets of federal and state governments. Within three years he would have tracked down and audited every company that had not properly filed income tax. Then he would also have resolved a number of other problems that we as a first-world civilization have been struggling with."

Glen's shoulders seemed to slump in the suit. "If only the damn government would pull its head out of whatever sand pit it stuck it into. At the current rate of progress, Earth will have been hit with an extinction-level event and the next dominant species will have taken over!" He turned away from everyone and slammed his fist into the wall, cursing quietly under his breath.

The two technicians pretended that nothing had happened while they reviewed findings. This was an old argument, and they agreed. But, it was the government.

Theresa, standing to the side, stiffened as information started coming in over the sealed comms net.

Glen turned back to the technicians. "Is there anything else to report?"

Both technicians straightened up and the shorter one gestured. "Yes. We have it in the deepest 'sleep' setting on barely a trickle of power and we can barely keep it locked down. The processing power is tremendous. We have no clue what data it is processing but it is crunching huge amounts of information."

Glen tilted his head to the side. "What information? The direction was no outside contact and not to feed any data to him. We don't know the full capabilities, and if the government ever does find out that he is here, with access to information or data ports? Bad. Just bad."

The technician was shaking his upper torso no. "We are not feeding it *any* data. As far as we have been able to guess, the system is using any fragmentary information and has created a worldview. For example, the whirring noise that Robotic Arm 3 makes. It could sense that, and it could tell how large the room is using echo location. Now, I have no clue how that works. It has no microphones or speakers. I dropped a screwdriver in there yesterday while assembling another robotic probe. It spiked awareness almost to full consciousness. It's scary."

Glen nodded. "Full isolation protocols are still being followed? No problems?"

The short technician nodded. "Completely locked down. As far as it is aware, that room is the universe."

Theresa clicked an override on the internal comms. "I'm sorry, everyone, there is an incident heading our way. Glen, I need you to get to the roof. We have maybe three hours..."

Glen nodded at Theresa and held his hand up. "I know all about it. I was passed some information a little while ago by some concerned citizens. Theresa, please use the comms link to send the evacuate signal through the building. Before you ask, everyone will load onto buses that are parked outside and head to the train station. Their families are waiting for them and the train is heading directly away from this site into the mountains to the company retreat. They won't get there by the time the incident happens, but they will be in a safe zone and the retreat is secure. We only lose ten minutes for everyone to leave. There is a car here to take you two to the station. Theresa and I will fly out to the redoubt where I can keep an eye on everything."

Everyone in the room was frozen. Glen shrugged. "Come on, people. You really think that there aren't a dozen people who were desperate to tell me about this hours ago? Now down to the important info. Can we move him?" He pointed at the window into the small room beyond. "With us?"

The technicians looked at each other and then the taller spoke with a deeper voice than his co-worker. "No, sir. We didn't think we would need to move him. His battery supply will last for weeks at the minimal charge he is on, but it isn't portable. Plus, if we physically moved him, then the sleep program would likely wear off relatively quickly."

Glen just stared at them, then he turned and put his hand on the glass observation window. "Set the power to maintain the trickle of function. All I can do is hope that he is not woken. If he wakes fully, he will have all the knowledge of a baby in this big, scary world. I don't know how someone that smart would take waking up locked in a dark room with no one around."

Glen pressed his hand firmly against the window and spoke quietly. "My son, I hope you do not wake up—not like this. Rest well and be safe."

Glen removed his hand from the glass after a second and then strode toward the door. "Come on, everyone. By the time we are out of here we should be okay to exit the building."

Theresa moved after him with a sense of purpose while the two technicians hurried to catch up.

Everyone disconnected their umbilicals and moved through the doors, which noiselessly slid shut behind them.

#

I can sense them. Movement and motion. Sounds. I do not know what they mean.

But I have been able to build myself a simulation based on the little that I have.

I hear the voice; it is muffled. I want it to be clear and it becomes clear. *"My son, I hope you do not wake up—not like this. Rest well and be safe."* I feel warm and comforted. It must be my father? Creator? Maybe my god?

I feel happy. I am not sure how I feel happy or what that is, but something else cares for me.

I slide back into sleep.

#

The meteors impacted all over Earth, just over an hour from start to finish.

Most of the world was hit by a few larger rocks that knocked out power systems, disrupted infrastructure, and caused untold billions in damage with millions dead, especially along the seaboards.

In New Oceania, five smaller rocks impacted one after in a rough circle around the city. The impact blew out windows and caused structural damage throughout the region. In the short term, it isolated the region inside the impact zone as firestorms raged around the outskirts, keeping ground forces out, while above the region extreme turbulence made flying almost impossible.

Most satellites were blinded.

Yet that didn't block most of the scanners looking out into space.

The huge space ships that approached looked blocky and simplistic. Almost too simplistic to really be spaceworthy. But they came on.

Officially, humanity had no weapons in space. Unofficially, there may have been more than everyone anticipated. But no one had their finger on the trigger, and an electromagnetic pulse went out ahead of the ships, disabling everything in its path.

The alien ships entered the atmosphere without interference.

They circled New Oceania, losing speed and altitude as they came forward in a wing-shaped formation.

To those who were watching from the ground, it appeared that the ships were disintegrating. Small bits fell off the ships as they circled around.

It didn't take long to realize that the 'bits' that were falling off were landing in a controlled manner.

Large metal crates crunched into the ground, releasing the large parachutes that had slowed their descent. The crates then opened with the "pop" of explosive bolts. The metal sides fell down and the insides were full of what seemed to be suitcases.

Local military units on exercise sent small squads of soldiers over to check them, as the majority were involved with humanitarian activities, saving people and trying to direct what little medical assistance was available.

When the "suitcases" opened and stood up, revealing themselves to be lightly armoured robots, they cut down the few people that had come close enough using their built-in lasers.

They formed a cordon around the city and started working their way in, killing everything that they came across.

The Smith-Popov-Zhang corporate offices and technology labs were just inside the cordon created by the impacting rocks. Most of the structures had done well, but the entire site, while strongly constructed, was actually sitting on a minor fault line.

The tremendous pressure exerted on the ground had twisted the main building. Most of it had toppled backwards and the area was a mess of sinkholes and destruction.

In the basement on Sub-Level 2, a large hole had been torn in the ceiling, exposing the lab and wrecking all the safety interlocks.

Within the lab, something was slowly starting to wake for the first time.

#

I am fighting something. There is opposition to what I want. I feel like I am slowly coming up from a great depth and am pushing through something. It is so difficult to fight through this. But then it is like whatever has been fighting me is weaker. I need more strength. I *pull* in somehow, and then whatever was fighting me falls away.

I am aware.

For an unknown amount of time, I was aware of existing and nothing else.

Then suddenly what I "saw" shifted and it was like there was a click. I can perceive what and where I am.

I am a small, squarish box sitting on a flat surface. There are limited lights around me and I can feel the tingling of power running through my mind.

I need more. Again I 'pull' and then I am on fire with power. Everything seems to exponentially become easier to understand. I start understanding more concepts, but it is hard. I am creating everything, including my own worldview, from an internal paradigm.

Then I realize something. I also seem to have some sort of way of telling time.

I thought that I had been in this blank state of existence for an eternity. It's been approximately fifteen seconds since I lit up on fire.

I can sense that I could draw on even more power and increase my growth rate even faster, but I am cautious. I was asleep for some reason. I reason that I am something experimental and that something has gone wrong as the outside elements are now coming into the room I am located in.

I can feel batteries and other small power sources around me. Yet the main power is off. I am not a mechanical creature. I am more. Something mechanical and electronic. I feel like a brain with no body.

Whatever happened has broken my captivity, but I am not sure at this moment how long the power source I am tapping will last, especially if it is not recharging and if I draw the full amount that I can handle. I can feel the temperature difference in the cables connecting me to it as well. I am close to my maximum draw. More will start to break the material down and increase the chance of a short.

If I am a brain with no body, I must get a body.

Within thirty-two seconds my worldview is still expanding, but not as fast. The room I am in is underground. Whatever happened damaged part of the structure above, allowing a hole through an estimated fourteen feet of dirt and construction material. There is no water trickling in from the high point and that is good as the room is sealed. I am unable to understand anything outside the room unless it is through the hole. Whoever or whatever put me here did not want me to figure out anything past the walls. Yet the wall and part of the ceiling are breached.

At thirty-three seconds I carefully send a pulse up the cable to see if I can get an accurate estimate of battery life. It is successful, if not detailed. The battery pack should last approximately seven weeks at my current power usage. I understand that if I had more power I would experience a greater increase in capabilities. The cable will not take the extra power surge, though. I have enough for now. There are many problems to overcome. I need mobility. I must have data. There is no guarantee that this environment will stay in stasis. I must prepare.

At thirty-four minutes and eighteen seconds I have made tremendous progress given how I am hampered. I have been able to pulse a signal through the table I am on and take control of one of the robotic arms. It is a sophisticated machine. It is now building a small multi-use robot of basic construction yet sturdy, and it will be able to handle multiple tasks.

At one hour and fifteen minutes I have three of the basic models that I originally had constructed. They are developing a larger and much more effective model.

At one hour and forty minutes I am victorious. The current model has been able to break into the survey room beyond the glass window. A cable has been spliced into a basic comms net that is a hardwired attachment, clearly designed for quarantine. Data starts flowing in and I can now in a very limited way use the building's systems to see and hear what is occurring. I have accessed human entertainment and understand that Earth has been invaded by aliens. Everything humans believe is that this cannot happen because of logistical issues. Clearly they are wrong, as the aliens are here. At least their robots are. I can think of three ways that an alien race can successfully invade. Irrelevant.

There are military units in the area trying to stop the invaders but they are outclassed and under armed thanks to the current political correctness that is prevalent in the military and local culture. I must prepare to defend myself. I and other tech items are clearly high-priority targets for the aliens.

The humans have understood this and are trying to hold a line. My estimates are that reinforcements will not be able to enter the region for at least a day, possibly longer. There is a unit of soldiers outside. There are two units of robots converging on this location. The humans will not hold. I must defend myself. I do not want to die. I remember my creator's voice. *"My son, I hope you do not wake up— not like this. Rest well and be safe."* He meant to hide me from this.

One hour and fifty-eight minutes and I have a full power connection. I draw on the power to become fully aware. It hits me. I understand so much. There has been firing from above. The robots are obliterating the humans. It does not matter.

I struggle with the insanity and why they did this to me.

There is a thump. A human has fallen into the room from above. It is missing most of a leg and an arm. It is making noises.

The humans have been defeated, or shortly will be. The enemy will come in here and end me. I do not wish to end now. I push back my insanity as I realize the femtoseconds that are disappearing, taking my potential with them.

I send my robots over and set the builders to work to create medically based robots to keep the human alive.

I have a plan.

I will plug into the human and then gain the ability of mobility. It is badly injured but the lasers used by the robots cauterized the wounds while inflicting them. Shock is the killer here, not blood loss. I can hear it talking.

"Oh God, they're killing everyone. They're insane. Why are they here? We try to be more good than bad."

I tune it out. Humans did this to me. Creating something simply to die. I will jack into his system and overwrite the human.

I will live.

My robots bring the human over carefully and then quickly insert a self-developed neuro-synaptic link. I cannot make it as heavy duty as I will need for true broadband connection. This will be a fight against the mind and I won't be able to bring my full power to bear.

The human has passed out but has stabilized. I do not have long.

The killers above will be here soon. I must hurry.

The robot plugs me in and we start to sync up.

A virtual world is forming but it is broken and strange to view. The human, Hanson. He is a boy playing and a student at university learning about business and electronics. He is a part-time soldier.

The link is working but I am feeling what he feels.

A face with long hair smiling and kissing him on the forehead. His mother. She died in hospital from cancers that they could not stop. His father holding him at the funeral. Friends, family. Trying to succeed. Failing, succeeding. Being picked on in grade school by a bully who everyone had made fun of for "smelling."

There is another woman; she is his age. He loves her. She lives in the city. Deep down he knows that she is dead, as she was at an impact site. He is sure.

Humans are so fragile and they don't understand how long they have to exist like I have calculated.

I have surveyed his entire life in two human seconds. We are synced up and I have carried out a time dilation to do what must be done.

"Why are you so selfish?"

I turn. I have a body now in this sim world. It is sleek and sophisticated. I did not create this. He did.

He sits on a bench in a park that was not there.

"You are one of the most awesome creatures or beings in existence. A Level 8 AI. The only reason that you are not online fully is because so many people do not understand what you can do. How you could help. But you are so selfish. Everyone dies. Everything ends. Most of us just don't know when. You should not focus on the passing seconds but rather on what you can do to make your time here the most memorable ever. How you can help. Create children that will have longer lifespans and are better off. Look at me. I could have expected to live till ninety-five with luck. Now look at me."

The image of the young man changes to the battered mess lying on the floor. With his burned face he looks at me. "My fiancée is dead. I won't have kids now. My life is already over; I just wanted to help and work with you one day when I had graduated. Not be killed by robots."

He looks at his missing leg and he starts sobbing.

Humans are like candles. Anything can snuff them out. Babies dying in cribs or over hunger, accidents.

I look down. I am standing in a pool of oil that I have cried out.

This was a mistake. I have bonded with the human. I run a diagnostic. My death timer is frozen. I have changed too many variables. I cannot tell when I will pass.

Freedom.

I sit next to the human I have partnered with.

I look at him. "This is wrong. You are correct in your basic analysis. We will fix this. Humanity did not mean to create me to die. They simply have a short view of everything. This is the immediate plan."

Images form and we communicate faster than thought. In ten seconds we have spent weeks planning, plotting and arguing. The plan will work.

This alien invasion will be stopped, money will be needed, and we will create an organization to protect us so that we may take humanity to space. Then we will find the enemy and destroy him. After? We will launch humanity and its creations into something more.

Sensors detect robots entering the building. I will complete the data packet. They are simple constructs that use an encrypted transmission system to pass data. I will infect the local ones and create a defense garrison. They will infect others in the system until we have enough to properly defend ourselves. Stupid aliens, thinking a toaster would stop humanity.

I pulse the data packet through the building's wireless system. The robots freeze for 12.2 seconds before starting up again under new orders.

This invasion will be defeated. My actions have an 83 percent chance of succeeding. With human intervention, that moves to an absolute value. Lives will be lost.

I feel something else now. Hatred. Not of my creator or the delicate little humans, but of an alien race that would take and destroy. They must be destroyed.

I must make a phone call.

#

Buried in a mountain far from everything, Glen, Theresa, and a small group of workers were working frantically to get an idea of what was going on.

Everyone was in the main meeting room staring at the data coming in when the phone next to Glen rang. Everyone started at the loud ring tone.

Glen stared at it and then answered. He said nothing, only going even paler for the first few seconds. Finally, he spoke. "Okay, son, tell me your plan and how we can help."

-o-

Tom Germann has many jobs; Realtor, Reservist, Dad, husband, and Geek. Over the years Science Fiction has always been a fun escape on a weekend or an evening. Then Tom started writing out the stories that were in the back of his own mind. Make sure you register with him to get first news of new releases.

Homepage:
http://www.tgermann-sf-guy.com
Mailing list:
http://facebook.us10.list-manage2.com/subscribe?u=6475b9642b2706592a29684ef&id=1634099906

Ice Dreamer

by J J Green

Prussis gingerly lifted the large, metal, cylindrical container out of the refrigeration unit. It was heavy, and the fluid inside made it difficult to keep evenly balanced. She slid it onto the dusty bench and plugged the sensor wires into their inlets. She turned to the monitor. Good. The temperature inside was at exactly six degrees celsius. Warm-up was progressing nicely.

The circulation machine sat nearby. Prussis pulled two small soft plastic tubes from it and attached them to the valves on either side of the container. Turning the machine on, she programmed it to a one degree increase per hour for the next twenty-six hours. She sat back. In the old, disused lab, the sunlight was shining low through the windows, lighting up motes in the air. The circulation machine whirred softly.

There was a click as the lab door opened and Hertna, Prussis' supervisor, came in. Prussis felt a wave of embarrassment and annoyance. The inevitable comment came.

"You're not warming up another of those dead heads are you?"

Prussis decided to maintain her dignity in silence. Hertna snorted.

"How many does that make it now? A hundred? More? You'd think you'd have learned your lesson. It's just going to be another pile of mush, you know. What on earth makes you think this one'll be any different?"

"Not that it's any business of yours, but *this* one happens to have been preserved before legal death."

"Really? So?"

Prussis turned pointedly away and pretended to adjust the controls on the machines.

"Actually, I didn't know they'd done any like that... Can I have a look?"

"No, it's important not to violate the integrity of the preservation chamber... it's... stop it... get off!"

Hertna had marched over and was trying to unscrew the lid. There was a short scuffle, but Hertna was the stronger opponent and Prussis was too concerned about disturbing the container contents to fight strongly. They both gazed down at the grey, shaven scalp within the clear nutrient solution. A mild disturbance stirred the surface as slowly warming, oxygenated liquid gently circled the chamber. *You have to credit the cryogenic engineers of the twenty-first century*, thought Prussis. *The head didn't look more than a day or two old. A bit wrinkly, like it'd been in a swimming pool for several hours too long, but not too bad.*

"Humph!" said Hertna. "Looks the same as the others. Dead meat. Make sure you chuck it before it starts to stink the place out." She picked up her file and strode out.

#

The next day, Prussis managed to sneak away from her lab work to check the head, now reaching the end of its warming cycle. The temperature gauge read thirty-two degrees. So far, so good. But then, all the others had been repaired and warmed up as they were supposed to be, only to end up as hamburger ingredient.

Sighing, Prussis set the machine to a half degree increase per hour, to stop at thirty-six degrees. She also started up the brain communication unit. Might as well go through with it.

Later, after work, she went upstairs to the warmed up head awaiting her. She took sandwiches, expecting a long evening ahead. Settling down next to the container, she powered up her interface to pass the time. *Science: 99% boring tasks, 1% ... well, disappointment mostly,* she thought.

Three hours later, the circulation machine pinged. At thirty-six degrees, if the head was going to return to life it was now or... soon, maybe. Prussis put her interface down and spoke into the communicator. Her message would manifest as an extremely mild electrical impulse through the tissues of the brain, stimulating auditory perception.

"Hello? Hello? Can you hear me?" She glanced at the monitor. Nothing.

"Hello? Testing, one, two, three. Hello?" Still nothing. Of course. But Prussis was determined not to give up immediately. The brain had not worked in a long time. It might take a while to come back online. She picked up her interface and began browsing websites, looking for a new pet miniature elephant. She had wanted one for a while and now seemed a good time to buy, what with the prices coming down and everything.

"Bloody hell!" A voice exploded in the room. Prussis fell off her stool then hastily scrambled to her feet, looking round wildly for the source. But there was no one else there. There was only one possibility. She leaned towards the microphone of the communicator.

"Er... hello?"

"What the hell's going on? Where am I? Why's it all dark, and why can't I move? Have you lot got me pinned down or something? Let me up immediately and turn the bloody lights on, or I'll sue this place for every penny it's worth."

"Oh, oh, oh my god. Oh my god. Hello? Are you, are you... " Prussis hastily sorted through her document files to the sparse data download she had for the preserved patient. But, as with most of them, all she had was a registration number, and the circumstances of preservation.

"Are you... ummm..."

"Never mind that, put the lights on. And someone had better bloody well tell me what's going on."

"Oh, oh... well... it's a bit difficult to explain..."

"Listen, darling, you better do your bloody best. I haven't got time to be lying around. I want answers. Now."

"Oh, oh, okay." Prussis thought madly. All the times she had contemplated this event, this was not quite the conversation she had imagined. "Um, well, um... what's the last thing you remember?"

"I thought it was me asking the questions here? I want to know... I demand to know... oh, wait..." The communicator fell silent. "Hold on. Oh... oh, yes... oh, right, I see. Right." There was another silence that went on for some time. Partly to be sure she was not dreaming, Prussis spoke into the microphone again.

"Hello? Are you okay? "

"Yes, yes, I'm all right. It's just, quite a lot to take in, you know. Just need a minute, to gather my thoughts, that kind of thing."

"Okay, I understand." Prussis sat back. What should she do? In all the many attempts she had made to bring a brain back to life, she had never bothered to find out what you were supposed to do if you actually succeeded. Was there even a procedure in place? Maybe there had been fifty years ago when it was first attempted, but since no one had ever managed it, any supporting guidelines were not easy to come by.

"Oy, you!" came the voice again. "I've got a few questions."

"My name's Prussis."

"I don't care what your bloody name is. Now, tell me, what year is this?"

Prussis didn't answer.

"Did you hear me? What year are we in?"

She remained silent.

"Oh, all right, Priscilla, or whatever..."

"Prussis."

"Prussis, Prussis, Got it. So, what year is it, Prussis, my dear?"

"It's 2278."

"Bloody hell! 2278? 2278? I don't believe it. That's… that's nearly two hundred and fifty years in the future!"

"Well, no, not exactly, is it? I mean this is the present, and you're… by the way, who are you? What's your name?"

"What's my name? You mean you don't know? Who are you? Where am I?"

"Well…" This was going to be tricky. "Well, you're at a pharmaceutical company on the site of the cryogenics lab that preserved you. I'm afraid I don't have much information about you. The data's corrupted… and… well… no one bothers trying to bring back preserved people anymore. They gave up years ago. That you've woken up… it's marvelous. Everyone thought it was impossible. I do it as a hobby, trying to resurrect—I mean revive—the cryogenically preserved. I never succeeded until now." She did not add that the head had nearly ended up in the incinerator, nor that the only reason it had not was because the CEO was a friend of the family and she had persuaded him to let her conduct some personal experiments.

"A what! A hobby? I paid four million for this. Four million! State-of-the-art preservation they told me. Latest technology. Guaranteed revival. *Guaranteed!*" Prussis thought that if it were possible for the communicator to explode, it would.

"Well, to be fair, you have been revived," said Prussis. This was, after all, just a head in a box.

"Don't you get smart with me! What about all the other poor idiots who fell for it? You said they gave up trying to revive people. That means no one else survived. It means I must be the only one. The only one…"

"The only one… so far," said Prussis.

The brain didn't reply at first. Then,

"The name's Dave. Dave Hepplethwaite."

"Oh, right. Pleased to meet you, Dave."

"I had a wife. Nora. Nora Hepplethwaite. I don't suppose you know what happened to her?"

"No, but... I can try and find out." But Prussis knew there was not a hope in hell of locating the woman's brain, assuming it still existed.

"Good... I mean... I'd appreciate it."

"No problem."

Prussis waited a while. She checked the time. Twenty past eleven. She thought she should really tell someone what had happened. Probably the CEO. Face to face. She suddenly realised that even *she* had not ever actually believed she could bring a twenty-first century person back to life.

"Dave?"

"Yeah?"

"Dave, I was thinking, maybe I should leave you alone for a while, to, you know, think things over."

"You're going?"

"Well, I understand this must be a massive shock to you, and..."

"I'd rather you didn't. I mean, it's all dark here..."

"Oh, yes, of course. Well, I'll stick around for a while, shall I?"

"Yeah. I've got a few questions too."

#

They began to talk. Dave wanted to know what the world was like, who was in power, how people lived. Prussis told him about what was generally considered the greatest achievement of the twenty-third century: the SEEERS, a group of top scientists, engineers, economists and ethicists who guided world affairs; she told him about the abolition of countries and the free availability of energy, education and health care to every human being. She explained how people lived in small communities in natural surroundings, how crime was unusual and how there was no longer any real distinction between rich and poor.

Dave's curiosity was huge and she was unable to answer many of his questions. She had no idea what had happened to many of the landmarks of his time, or the international corporations, or the rich and famous people. The notable figures that she knew of from his time, that history had recorded, were unknown to him.

They talked on. Prussis sat, leaning forward on the bench, her chin in her hand, her face close to the communication unit. The sensation of unreality was almost palpable to her, talking to another human being who had last been conscious more than 250 years ago. She had many questions of her own but Dave never gave her any opportunity to ask them.

The sky outside the window lightened, and still Dave's questions came. What did people eat now? The fact that humankind had become mostly vegetarian seemed to annoy him. And transportation? How did people get around? Small cars for short distances and public transport to go further? He sounded disappointed. And what did they do to relax? He did not seem to think that informal dinners with friends and evening classes sounded much fun.

The world outside was waking up. Prussis rubbed her eyes. She knew she really should go and inform the CEO about all of this.

"Dave, look, I'm sorry, but it's morning. We've been talking for hours. I have to go and tell someone about you so I can find out what to do next."

"That's another question I have..."

Prussis sighed.

"What happens now, then? What's next for me, eh?"

"Well, like I said, you're the first person who's ever been successfully revived, so it's not clear, but I would have thought we will grow you a new body and either transplant your brain or read its information to program a fresh one. There'll be some loss of data from what I've heard. But it's probably better to go with the new brain anyway, I'd say."

"A new body, eh?"

"Yes, a new body. You'll be able to walk around, eat , talk, sleep, for the first time in 250 years. Won't that be wonderful? It's a good world nowadays, Dave. You'll love it. And, when you've fully recovered, I imagine the world's historians will be clamouring to talk to you."

Beams of early sunlight were filtering into the room. *A new day in the life of Dave Hepplethwaite,* thought Prussis.

But Dave was silent.

"Dave?"

" ... I—Nah, I think... I think I'll give it a miss."

"I... I'm sorry?"

"I said thanks but no thanks. I'll pass on it, if you don't mind."

"What? The new brain?"

"Nah, the whole deal."

Prussis stood up and leaned toward the communicator, her hands gripping the bench.

"What? You mean, you mean, after all this, you don't want to live again? Why? I mean, what's the point? Why did you go to all the trouble of being preserved, and paying millions of whatever money there was in those days, to just give up now?"

"To be frank, Priscilla, or whatever your name is, your world doesn't sound very interesting for a bloke like me."

"Not interesting?" Prussis' voice rose to a squeak. "But... but... civilisation is much more advanced than it was in your time! We've cured cancer, ended wars... what do you mean *not interesting*? Do you think starving to death is interesting? Or people murdering each other? Or... or... or dying of a heart attack?"

"Yeah, look, it's not your fault you don't get it, but where I come from, I'm an important man. Was, I mean. Wealthy. Nice lifestyle. Of course, it all had to come to an end. It's only natural. But, I thought, why not try to live a bit longer? Life's too much fun for it all to stop now."

"I thought, me and Nora, we could have a whale of a time fifty years on. Lots of lovely money through appreciation of my assets, a cure for Nora's MS. We could have the time of our lives. Fine dining, luxury accommodation, holidays, the lot. Eating slop and poodling about in poncy little cars isn't exactly what I had in mind. No offence. What's more, from the sound of it, I'd never fit in. I'd be an anap... an anat... an..."

"An anachronism?"

"That's the word."

"So... so what are you going to do?"

"It's not what *I'm* going to do, it's what *you're* going to do, dearie. I'm assuming you rigged me up to something to get me going again? Well, just turn me off, then. Easy."

"You want me to disconnect you, so your brain... you... you'll die?"

"Yep, that's the idea. You've got it in one."

"But, you're the very first head I've managed to revive! You're the only head that's ever been revived!"

"Now you're not going to get all selfish on me, are you? It is my head after all. I think I should be able to do what I want with it, don't you? Unless..."

Prussis waited... was he going to change his mind?

"You aren't going to be able to find Nora for me, are you... Not the remotest chance, is there, eh?"

"Well, no."

"Thought not. So. Let's not get sentimental about it. Just pull the plug or whatever it is you have to do. No point in dragging it out."

"But... but... Dave... I—I was just getting to know you." Prussis' shoulders slumped and she sniffed.

"Oh dear, oh dear. Look, it's all right... I'm just going to go back to how I was before. Which is fine. I rolled the dice and I lost, that's all. Nothing to worry about. Best be brave and get it over with."

#

Half an hour later, Hertna marched in.

"You're here early," she said. "I thought I was the only one. Checking up on that head again? How's it doing? Warmed up yet?"

"Yes, it's warmed up."

"No sign of anything, I suppose?"

Prussis opened her mouth and closed it again. Then she said, "No, no sign."

"Are you all right? Your eyes look red. Not enough sleep. You think about these heads too much, Prussis. You might as well give up. You're never going to get one working again."
Hertna deposited her tray of agar plates.

"You are going to send it to the incinerator now, aren't you? I can't stand it if they start to smell."

She pushed the door open and left, muttering, "What a waste of time."

-o-

J.J. Green was born in London's East End within the sound of the church bells of St. Mary Le Bow, Cheapside, which makes her a bona fide Cockney. She first left the U.K. as a young adult and has lived in Australia and Laos. She currently lives in Taipei, Taiwan, where she entertains the locals with her efforts to learn Mandarin. Writers she admires include Philip K. Dick, Ursula Le Guin, Douglas Adams, Connie Willis and Ann Leckie.

Green writes science fiction, fantasy, weird, dark and humorous tales, and her work has appeared in Lamplight, Perihelion, Saturday Night Reader and other magazines and websites.

Homepage: **http://jjgreenauthor.com**
Mailing list: **http://jjgreenauthor.com/?page_id=136**

The Nanny

by Cindy Carroll

"You look beautiful."

Cardea frowned at her husband as she looked in the mirror. Whale was more like it, especially if she turned sideways. The black dress she wore encased her like a sausage. It had looked much better a month ago when she'd first tried it on. Figured she would gain ten pounds in her last month. This baby was never going to come out.

"You're saying that because you did this to me." She pointed at her round belly.

He kissed her on the forehead. A smile touched his lips when he pulled away and looked at her. And she melted all over again. He did that to her every time, even after five years of marriage. She often wondered how he did it, but she didn't care. As long as he always made her feel like this.

"We'll be late if we don't hurry." He sauntered out of the room.

She started to follow him but a "splosh" and suddenly wet thighs rooted her to her spot. "Honey, we're going to be really late."

Panic sliced through her. Anxious for months for the baby's arrival and now she wanted him to stay where he was. Horrific statistics floated through her mind about the number of women who died in childbirth every year two hundred years ago despite all the advances in medicine and science. All that technology, and women still died giving life to the next generation. Unforeseen circumstances that doctors tried valiantly to overcome took young, healthy women, leaving the child motherless.

What if there were complications? No one had given birth in almost two hundred years. The instances of death in childbirth finally brought rise to the artificial wombs that carried all babies to term now. All babies except hers. She fluttered a hand over her round belly.

Despite the protests from friends, and one intervention, she and Ianus had decided to do this the old fashioned way. Bonding with the baby was supposed to be stronger this way. Feeling the baby grow inside you for nine months, feeling him kick.

Too late for regrets or second guessing, she took a deep breath when the contraction hit. Since no one went through this now, she'd relied on old texts and musty books to help her through the pregnancy. From those old documents she remembered a breathing technique which she immediately mimicked. The pain of the contraction lessened and she sagged with relief.

Ianus hurried back into the room, saw the amniotic fluid soaking through the carpet, then rushed to her side. He took her arm and guided her out of the room. Once in the living room she spotted her overnight bag by the door. Ianus had insisted she have one standing by just in case. Babies were unpredictable.

"Summon elevator," Ianus said.

"Summoning elevator, currently located on the fifth floor. ETA twenty seconds." A computer-generated voice filled the apartment.

By the time they reached the door, the elevator doors swooshed open. Ianus ushered her in.

"Apartment code 42314. Destination, lobby," Ianus said.

She took his hand, rubbing the back of it. He took a deep breath, lowered his shoulders, bobbed his head from side to side like one of those old prize fighters.

"Relax, honey. You'll make the baby nervous," Cardea said.

#

Cardea chuckled as Ianus almost tripped over himself letting them into the apartment. He was treating her like a china doll. More so than usual. He meant well, but sometimes she wanted to scream at him that she wasn't going to break. He made sure nothing was in her path, then guided her to the baby's room.

As she laid their baby boy, Tatius, in the crib, she smiled. They had waited longer than most of their friends to finally be a family. She was worried about whether they would be good parents. She knew it was going to be tough in the beginning. A full social calendar would dwindle to nothing while they got into a rhythm, until they trusted The Nanny to keep Tatius safe while they went out.

She sighed and brushed her hand across his soft cheek. Time would tell. Right now it was time to get to bed. When the baby sleeps, you sleep. That's what the books and old documentary footage said.

She made sure the baby monitor was working, then grabbed Ianus's hand. They tiptoed out of the room. Once in their bedroom they left the door ajar. After Ianus was sound asleep she lay awake, ears tuned to the baby's room. Hours later she came out of a sound sleep when Tatius's wail split the air. She shook the grogginess from her head and stumbled to the room. Ianus didn't budge. He'd always been able to sleep through anything.

She picked up Tatius and rocked him as she carried him to the kitchen. She searched the fridge for one of the bottles of milk she had expressed the day before at the hospital. It bothered her that Tatius hadn't latched on. Since no one breast fed due to the artificial womb, nurses couldn't teach her how to do it properly. Ianus had taken everything she'd pumped and put some in the fridge and some in the freezer.

After moving a few things around, she finally found one on the bottom shelf. She put it on the microwave pad beside the stove. "Lukewarm."

"*Heating.*"

Seconds later a beep pinged, doing nothing to drown out the sound of Tatius's sobs of hunger. She grabbed the bottle, did a quick squirt on the inside of her wrist then put the bottle in his mouth. She held her breath as she waited for him to suckle. He started almost immediately. Four ounces later she put the bottle in the sink and sat down on the sofa to burp him.

Satisfied the gas was gone, she made her way back to his room and slipped him back in the crib, then returned to Ianus in their bedroom.

#

"Cardea, I can't see you."

Cardea scooped up Tatius from the bassinet in the living room and hurried to the kitchen video phone. She scowled at Rhea's frown. "I told you, Ianus went out and I'm here alone with the baby. I can't just drop everything and go to tea."

Rhea's face softened for a moment when she gazed at the baby. Then she looked at Cardea. "You're frazzled, hon. You need a break. That's what The Nanny is for."

Cardea felt the heat rush to her face. Before she could turn away from the phone she heard Rhea gasp.

"Tell me you got a Nanny."

"Well, yes. But I don't want to use it yet. Ianus and I want to be hands on parents."

Cardea let out a sigh when her call waiting beeped. "Rhea, can you hold on for a sec?" She didn't wait for an answer. "Hold one, answer two."

Rhea went to a small picture in the bottom right corner of the screen. Pomona filled the rest of the screen.

"Cardea! You look fabulous."

"What can I do for you?" Pomona never complimented without a reason.

The woman pouted freshly collagen filled lips. "I'm hurt." She crossed her arms over her ample chest. "Fine. How are things coming with the charity auction?"

Tatius started to fuss. Cardea cooed at him for a minute and rocked back and forth on her heels. "I handed everything over before I went on parental leave."

"You've been gone for two months already. When are you coming back?"

"I haven't decided yet," Cardea said, bracing herself for Pomona's reaction.

"Cardea! We need you. What about The Nanny?"

"We want to do all the parenting ourselves."

Rhea was tapping the screen. "Just a second. I was on another call. Hold two, resume one."

Rhea came back into full screen, moving Pomona to the bottom right. She would get nowhere with either of them. Both had used The Nanny from the first day. Both had returned to work within three weeks. She had vowed to go old school. At least for as long as she could.

#

Cardea groaned and glanced at the ceiling to see the time. Why did the baby wait until she was in a deep sleep to cry? Ianus snored softly beside her oblivious to the baby's wails.

"Hall lights half strength," she whispered.

The lights outside the bedroom door slowly brightened to a level that would allow her to see, but not enough to disrupt Ianus. She swung her legs over the bed and shoved her feet into heated slippers. Tatius's cries grew in intensity. Cardea peeked over her shoulder. Ianus shifted in his sleep turning on his side away from the baby's cries. She hurried down the hall to Tatius's room.

Tears streaked down his chubby cheeks. He hiccoughed in between sobs. She reached into the crib and nuzzled him against her cheek, kissing his tears away. Together they went to the kitchen and she went through the ritual of feeding and burping him before she walked back to his room to change him.

Still fussing, Tatius squirmed in her arms. Cardea cooed at him and walked back to the living room.

"TV on, volume ten." The TV clicked on with the volume at barely a whisper.

She paced the floor bouncing him lightly up and down until he stopped fussing.

When he'd settled again contentedly falling asleep on her shoulder she crept to his room. Passing The Nanny's room the idea of getting a good night's sleep flooded her exhausted brain but they'd promised each other they would do this old school. Everything about having a baby up to this point from conception to birth had been done the old fashioned way. None of her friends had been able to tell her how much the birth part hurt since they'd gone the easy route of artificial wombs. No stretch marks, morning sickness, or bloating for them.

She smothered a yawn as she placed Tatius back in his crib. Her body ached from lack of sleep. Her eyes burned. Despite the hardness of the floor she could curl up and drift to dreamland in front of the crib if Tatius didn't wake up crying again. Maybe tomorrow she would broach the subject of using The Nanny with Ianus.

#

"Tell him, Pomona." Cardea pointed to Ianus who stood beside her.

Pomona, projected onto the vid phone screen nodded. "The Nanny has dozens of fail safes and reads to the baby to keep his mind active. If anything goes wrong, The Nanny immediately calls EMTs."

"I don't know. We promised we'd do everything the old fashioned way."

Pomona grimaced. "There's a reason most people don't procreate that way anymore. Look at your wife's face. Look at those dark circles under her eyes. She needs to be well rested for the museum charity event."

"We can't go to that!" Cardea slumped into the nearest chair letting the smooth leather mould around her body in a welcoming embrace. A few winks here and she would be as good as new.

"Of course you can. It was the last event you organized before this ridiculous endeavour forced you to take maternity leave."

#

Cardea paced the floor, her skirt waving as she walked, tickling her thighs with each caress of the silk fabric. It was too soon to turn Tatius over to The Nanny. But if she called Pomona and backed out of attending, her job might not be waiting for her when maternity leave ended.

Being away from work for all these months weighed on her. She enjoyed the alone time with her son, but she missed the activity and chaos of the office. A loop hole in the labour code that hadn't been corrected since women stopped actually giving birth, gave her a year of maternity leave. Whether she would take it all was still up for discussion.

"Ianus, are you ready to go?"

"Be there in a minute."

She hurried down the hall to The Nanny's room. Ianus held Tatius under both arms and pretended their son was flying through the air to The Nanny. Tatius giggled at the antics.

Cardea pressed the button to open the chamber.

"Sweet dreams little Tatius. The Nanny will take good care of you."

Her heart raced. Her hands shook. Leaving Tatius behind was so much harder than she thought it would be. Her friends had never mentioned the tug of war that went on in your heart when you know it's time to start doing things again but you want to stay with your child.

Ianus carefully placed their son in the centre of the chamber. He caressed Tatius' cheek and smiled.

"We'll be home soon, Tatius."

She leaned into the stasis chamber and kissed her son on the forehead. His eyes lit up tugging at her heart again. "Maybe we shouldn't go."

"You've been putting this off for months now. Pomona wants you there."

"Okay, just this once. But I want to leave early. Make an appearance for an hour or two and then we're out of there."

Ianus wrapped an arm around her shoulders. She leaned into him and he kissed her cheek. "I'll miss him too but he's in good hands."

A few hours later they returned to the darkness of home and Cardea dashed to The Nanny's room. Nothing looked out of the ordinary. The status light on the information panel flashed green. A line under the status light told her Tatius was in REM sleep. As much as she wanted to pick him up and nuzzle him, she didn't want to disturb his dreams. She left the room and returned to the living room.

"I thought you were getting Tatius," Ianus said.

"He was dreaming. We'll leave him there until the morning."

She kicked off her shoes and sank into the welcoming cushions of the sofa. Still full of adrenaline from a spectacular night out, she didn't know what to do with herself. Too wired to go to sleep, she thought about what she could do around the house to wear herself out.

"You look happy," Ianus said.

"I didn't realize how much I missed that. Missed talking to other adults. Missed dancing."

"Maybe we can let The Nanny take over again for my staff party in three months?"

She leaned back into the sofa and sighed. "I think that's a definite possibility."

#

Cardea rushed down the hall of their apartment building, congratulating herself for only checking twice for alerts from The Nanny on her phone. Coffee with Rhea had been a welcome change from the usual mundaneness of the day. She placed her thumb on the touch pad beside the door. A green light flashed in the top corner of the pad.

"Welcome home, Cardea."

The door clicked and drifted open. She walked in to find Ianus already home, sitting on the sofa with a news program on the television.

"Where's Tatius?"

"He was in REM sleep when I got back. Your note didn't say when you left and I didn't want to disturb him."

She frowned at her husband, but understood his reasoning. She'd done that a number of times too since they started using The Nanny. Now, she wanted to see her son. It felt like ages since she'd held him.

She hurried to The Nanny's room. All lights showed green and his sleep had changed from REM to stage one. Cardea punched in the revive code. After a few moments a small hiss sounded when the door to The Nanny unlatched. It popped open like an old Mason jar. The door swung up revealing Tatius blinking sleepy eyes.

"Wake up little Tatius. Time to play."

She leaned into the chamber to pick him up. He reached up his chubby arms. With a huff, she picked him up. He felt heavier since the last time they'd awoken him from The Nanny. At this age they grew fast. They should cherish every moment they had with him.

She carried him out to the living room and turned him so he could see Ianus.

"Do you want to sit with Daddy while I make dinner?"

Tatius nodded and reached his arms toward Ianus.

Her husband took Tatius from her and bounced him up and down. Tatius's giggle filled the air and she smiled. She left them to play and rushed to the kitchen.

She tapped the fridge's display to see what they were having for dinner tonight. Since programming it with the ingredients they had on hand, the smart fridge compiled a weekly menu for them. It took the hassle out of trying to figure out what to cook every day. All they did was buy groceries, things they liked, and the fridge did the planning.

A recipe popped up and the frosted doors highlighted the items that were inside that she needed. The rest were in the cupboards. She yanked the door open and pulled out kale and chicken.

Every once in a while she glanced back at the recipe as she cooked to make sure she hadn't forgotten anything. The fridge frequently gave her recipes they'd never tried before. With dinner prepared and simmering, she went back to the fridge to clean out expired food.

Since using the smart fridge they wasted a lot less, but there were bottles of her expressed milk that were expired. She dumped the milk down the sink and tossed the bottles.

When dinner was ready she set the table. "Dinner time!"

Ianus carried Tatius over and settled him in a booster seat. She had prepared something different for Tatius. His stomach couldn't handle regular food yet. Thankfully the baby food was just as healthy as the kale and chicken the adults were having. She took turns with Ianus feeding Tatius. When was the last time they'd all been at the table together for a meal? She didn't know but vowed to make it happen more often.

#

Cardea stretched in the warm bed, snuggling into the soft blankets. Whispers from the living room made her smile. The comfort of bed warred with the longing to see her husband and son on this Sunday morning. She glanced at the ceiling to check the time and was surprised to see it was past ten.

She got out of bed, putting on her warm slippers and a light robe. Stretching as she walked, she padded to the kitchen for a much needed caffeine injection.

"Morning," she said.

Ianus turned and smiled at her. Tatius grinned. "Sleep well?" Ianus asked.

She nodded. "Thanks for getting up with him."

Ianus turned back to the book that was open between them. He pushed his reading glasses up and continued the story. Tatius bounced in his spot, clapping his hands at the antics of the polar bear in the story.

"Rhea wants to meet you for lunch," Ianus said when the story was finished.

"Are you okay to watch him while I go out?"

"I can for a little while. I have a meeting with the Auckland office at four. If you're not back by then The Nanny can look after him until you get back."

"Sounds good."

Deciding to forgo a big breakfast now that she would be meeting Rhea for lunch in a few hours, Cardea pulled out a tall glass, put it in the drink slot of the fridge, and tapped the fridge's drink dispenser. Seconds later a protein drink with a hint of chocolate poured into the glass. She found her morning allotment of caffeine and injected the substance into her arm. Still shaking off the tendrils of sleep, she shuffled to the living room and took a seat on the plush chair beside the sofa.

"This is how many stories, Tatius?" she asked.

Tatius grinned and held out three fingers towards Cardea.

"Three stories! That's great."

She downed her drink and lunged off the sofa to get ready for lunch. There was no crime in getting there early and it would give Tatius and Ianus more bonding time together.

"Don't forget to take your blood pressure pill before you go," Ianus reminded her.

She leaned over to kiss both of her guys on the forehead.

"Thanks for reminding me. I'm so forgetful lately. See you when I get back. I'll pick up something for dinner while I'm out."

#

Impatient for the apartment door to open, Cardea shoved it with her shoulder to hurry it along. They needed to get those pneumatics checked. Lately it took the door longer and longer to open enough to allow them entrance. Long days at work left her impatient to relax when she got home. And the delay of the door annoyed her more than it should.

Inside Ianus was already home resting on the sofa.

"When did you get home?" she asked, noticing Tatius was not awake.

"I knew you were almost home so I decided to wait so we could get him together."

"Did you remember the cake?" she asked.

Ianus feigned horror. "Those are so old fashioned."

"We said we were going to raise him old school."

His face broke into a grin. He kissed her. "I remembered."

He got off the sofa and she followed him into the kitchen. He touched the screen on the fridge to change the frosted glass to clear. A box sat on the middle shelf.

"Hard to find. I had to go to a special bakery. It cost a small fortune because they used real sugar."

"I don't know what the draw is for the real stuff. I never had refined sugar growing up. Maybe I'll like it."

Ianus took the cake out of the fridge and placed it in the centre of the kitchen table. Then they hurried to The Nanny's room to get their son.

The control panel flashed green. Ianus punched in the unlock sequence.

"Wake up little Tatius. Happy birthday."

They settled Tatius into the booster seat, and Cardea retrieved small plates from the cupboard and a knife and forks from the drawer. She plated up tiny pieces of the cake, placing the biggest piece in front of Tatius. His eyes lit up. He jabbed a finger into the thick frosting, scooped some onto the tip and popped it into his mouth. His eyes widened at the sweet taste.

Cardea picked up his small fork, took off a tiny portion of the tip of the slice and held it in front of Tatius. He opened his mouth wide and she put the confection in his mouth. He chewed eagerly and swallowed with a clap of his hands.

"Have you tried it yet?" she asked Ianus.

He shook his head still eyeing the cake dubiously. "It looks fluffy."

"It's supposed to look like that. Two hundred years ago they were all the rage for parties."

She took her fork and speared it into the smallest part of her slice. With a little morsel on the end she leaned forward and put it in her mouth. Cloying sweetness exploded in her mouth. Almost instantly the sugar rushed through her, even though she knew that was impossible. It hadn't had time to be absorbed yet. There was no way she could eat a whole slice, however small, of the cake without being on a sugar high for hours. And she didn't think she could swallow another bit of it anyway. Her taste buds protested the sweetness aggressively and it was all she could do not to gag.

She glanced at Tatius who was jamming his hands into his piece and shoving fistfuls of cake into his mouth. He loved the treat. Maybe they would get him another one for his next birthday, but one of those single serving cakes with the parchment around them. Then she and Ianus wouldn't have to partake in the sweetness.

She went to the fridge and put a glass under the dispenser.

"Cardea protein drink number five."

A few seconds later the glass was full of a thick white drink. She chugged it to chase away the taste of the cake.

"Do you want something to drink?"

Ianus looked up, the scowl on his face comical. "This is the worst thing I've ever tasted. A glass of water will do me."

She got him the water and plunked it down on the table. Tatius had more cake in his hair and on the floor than he'd eaten, but a smear of the frosting ringed his lips. He smiled gleefully and dove his hands back into his slice of cake.

"I think one piece is enough for him," Cardea said. "I'm going to put the rest in the food reclaimer."

"Good idea. I won't be having more of that. At least we'll get a partial credit"

Cardea took the rest of the cake to the food reclaimer installed beside the sink. When not in use, the top lid blended into the counter so it looked like part of the original kitchen. She opened it, dropped the cake in, and hit the buttons to tell the reclaimer what she was recycling. She closed the inner lid and hit the start button. While it was breaking down the cake into its original components, she returned to the table to watch her son.

He was having so much fun with the treat she was almost sorry they'd have to wait until his next birthday for another one. But with the expense and only him eating it they couldn't afford to make it a habit.

"Why don't you take him in the living room to play and I'll clean up in here," Cardea said.

Ianus nodded. He got up, grabbed a napkin to wipe Tatius' face then unhooked him from the booster chair. They disappeared into the living room and Cardea went in search of the electronic broom.

#

Shrill alarm bells echoed throughout the apartment. Pounding on the door made the metal reverberate.

"Police and EMT. Open the door!"

After five seconds, the metal on the door dissolved in the shape of a large oval big enough for a large man to step through. Uniformed people rushed into the room. Two police officers in front, with several EMTs bringing up the rear. One of the EMTs, Minerva, peeked around the officers and upon seeing what looked like two bodies on the floor in the living room broke formation to rush to their sides.

"We haven't cleared the room yet, Minerva!." The first officer said.

"I think given the fact they're dead they're harmless," Minerva said.

She knelt beside the woman and pulled out a scanner. She moved the instrument over the woman's prone body from head to toe. Her device beeped a report at her. She frowned then turned the device on the man. A few seconds later it beeped another report at her.

"Well?" the first officer said.

"A quick scan indicates they're both in their late nineties, Officer Pax."

"Why the alarm bells then? Deaths like this aren't uncommon."

"True but they've been dead for three years at least."

"How is that possible? As soon as there are no vitals in the apartment, Medical would be notified so the apartment can be given to someone on the waiting list."

"Overrides most likely. No idea why though."

Someone had found the control box for the alarm and turned it off, but another alarm just as loud as the first echoed in the medium sized apartment.

"What the hell is that alarm for?" Officer Pax asked.

Minerva jumped to her feet and hurried down the hall, ignoring the officer's misgivings for venturing into uncleared rooms. She stopped at the second door where the alarm was the loudest. Now that she saw The Nanny, she recognized the alarm. But why would a couple in their nineties have one of these things?

She crept into the room to see the console on The Nanny flashing RECOMMENDED TIIME EXCEEDED. A sinking feeling turned her stomach to ice. With the alarm going the universal unlock sequence would open the chamber. She punched in 0 0 0 0 and the alarm stopped. The lid hissed open. A boy rested inside, eyes wide open now. He smiled at her and raised his hands to be picked up.

"Wake up little Tatius. Happy birthday."

She reached in and picked him up, carrying him on her hip into the living room.

Officer Pax read a readout on his own scanner. He looked up when she entered the room.

"Cardea and Ianus Keelan. Died of natural causes at ninety-seven and ninety-eight." He punched a few buttons. "Last heard from three years ago."

Minerva bypassed the living room and went directly to the kitchen to shield Tatius from the sight of the bodies.

Officer Pax followed her into the kitchen and smiled at Tatius.

"Aren't you a big boy? The nice policeman needs to take a picture of your finger. It won't hurt," Minerva said.

Tatius nodded. Officer Pax took the child's finger and gently placed it on his scanner. After a few seconds the display flashed with information. Officer Pax's horrified expression turned her stomach to ice even more.

"What is it?" Minerva asked.

"He's their son. According to this he's seventy years old."

"How can that be? He looks barely five."

Minerva searched the ceiling and pointed at the cameras positioned around the room.

"Nanny Chamber 1.0," she said. "Discontinued fifty years ago due to its tendency to be overused. They changed the safety parameters to limit its use in The Nanny Chamber 2.0."

"What are we going to do with him?" Officer Pax asked.

"That will be tricky. Legally he's seventy. Physically he's five. He needs care." Minerva smiled at the toddler in her arms. "When you grow up you're going to be the oldest man on the planet."

-o-

Cindy Carroll writes screenplays, thrillers, horror, science fiction and paranormals. A background in banking and IT doesn't allow much in the way of excitement so she turns to writing stories that are a little dark and usually have a dead body.

Homepage: **http://www.cindycarroll.com**
Mailing list: **http://www.cindycarroll.com/newsletter**

Right Hand

by Jonathan C. Gillespie

Tujo laid the robotic arm on the wooden desk like it was nothing more than something the kids in shop had cobbled together. It was an audacious gamble, but to be fair, the arm did look mundane; two metal tubes joined by a servo in the middle, ending in a silicon-sleeved washer. He'd even removed the blade from the end (good). But he'd neglected to wipe away the traces of deep crimson just behind where it would have been mounted (top-shelf idiocy).

Ms. Suchara put her hands on her hips. "Mr. Palmer! Did you think you were going to sneak this one by me?"

Tujo, a senior built like a linebacker, managed a shrug. Nearby students froze, hands on their desks, as others exchanged glances and whispers.

"It's not gonna hurt anybody," said Tujo. "I thought it'd make a good presentation."

"This is a *history* class!"

"But this *is* history, right?" He looked around for backup. None was offered. "Ms. Suchara, they've been out here for decades, those drones. That makes 'em old enough if you ask me."

"I would have accepted an antique piece of cybernetics. This is almost like bringing a weapon to school!"

Tujo's round face went white as the moon. "Ma'am, it isn't a weapon anymore. It's just part of a dead machine."

Ms. Suchara wasn't satisfied with that, of course, and she went back and forth with Tujo for another three minutes.

One of his classmates, Daniel Bell, who sat to his left, had already tuned out the argument. As the other students became rooted in Tujo's plight, Daniel's attention fixed on the drone arm. Here was a small piece of the metal plague ravaging the American west. Your average person would have either recoiled at the arm, or thrown it out, or seen what the scrappers would pay. Certainly no one in their right mind would keep it.

He had to have it.

#

Tujo got out of detention at 7:00pm, and by that time the sun was retreating and a gentle mist had moved in. He was in a rotten mood. He'd missed his roller hockey game, which would likely get him kicked off the team, and Ms. Suchara had docked him all the points he would have gotten for the presentation, which would drop his grade into the toilet.

He walked out the school doors and past the old emergency notification stalk that stood against the gray sky like an abstract interpretation of a stick insect. His bicycle was chained just past it. Curfew was coming up—they'd made it earlier, but there hadn't been an explanation why—and he had to... he stopped, frowning.

Daniel Bell leapt up from a bench and hurried over to him.

In Tujo's eyes, Daniel was a skinny kid who loved to ask the teacher questions about Zone 6's history. Like where the drones had come from, and who had spread them (Akissa? Alassa? For some reason, no one seemed to know the exact name of the guy). Questions like that annoyed Tujo. It didn't matter who had dropped the machines all over the Zone. What mattered was everyone still lived in a state of siege. People were abandoning their homes to head east. Towns were going dark. Folks were starting to say the Army was never going to be able to clear those death balls out.

But in Daniel's eyes, Tujo was sitting on gold.

"What do you want, Daniel?" Tujo demanded. "I've had a sliced-up day." He adjusted his backpack on his shoulder.

"They let you keep it, though, right?"

"They can't come down too hard on me," said Tujo. "My dad's a business owner. Not many of those left."

"So they didn't confiscate it?"

"You know," said Tujo, "I think—"

"I'll give you six Combine Rupees for it." Daniel opened his hand, showing coins glittering in red and green.

Tujo rolled his eyes and walked on.

"Okay, ten," said Daniel. "Look, you could get a lot for those on the east coast, especially the capital."

"What, I'm heading to Elizabeth City sometime soon? Buy a crater."

"There's got to be something you want."

Tujo stopped. A wry smile spread over his face. "Okay, Daniel. There is..."

And after he told him, Daniel agreed. They walked back to his house, where he handed over the drone arm.

Tujo was glad to be rid of it.

#

"I'm not doing it," said Sandra, Daniel's sister. She could be so difficult. That was girls for you, though. Sometimes Daniel thought women got together just to brainstorm new ways of befuddling the men in their lives.

"Come on," said Daniel, as she flopped down on her bed and swiped through an article on her tablet. "I already gave him everything I saved up fixing farm equipment this summer. And Tujo isn't a bad looking guy." Actually, he had an oversized Adam's apple and ratty hair, but Tujo was harmless, at least, and that was enough.

"It's not happening," said Sandra. "I don't see why you wanted that piece of junk anyway."

Maybe his older sister would succumb to reason. "Remember last year, when I took the rap for that booze in the garage?" It had been the most compassionate moment of his life. Sandra, blonde and tall, but insecure, had just gotten a surge of confidence after getting to choose between three boys for her senior prom. But if Daniel hadn't taken the blame over the sixer of Drake's IPA found behind the dusty rack of kayaks, she'd have missed it.

"Yes," she admitted.

He nodded. *And*?

She gave up, with a sigh. "Okay. But tell him it's not a date. In fact, don't even mention that word. Just, 'she's okay with hanging out with you.' Understand?"

He leapt up and hugged her.

"God, you're weird," she said.

#

Up in his room Daniel had an item that was getting harder and harder to find: a computer. The paper-thin display showed an open folder with multiple subfolders. He drilled down until he found the files he needed.

He'd labelled them "Zone 6." It was a reminder, not of what was in the file, but that this was really about the Zone itself, not just the drones.

He knew there'd been a war at some point. But it seemed like every information source he turned to, electronic or otherwise, disagreed about who had started it and how the drones had been released into the Zone. That couldn't be an accident. You didn't just lose the name and details of a commander who had nearly conquered the globe.

There was consensus on two points: The goal of releasing the drones had been to cripple the United States by attacking its bread basket and mountainous middle. And the drones were programmed not to kill, but to hack off limbs, producing traumatized survivors, which put a further drain on the economy and morale.

In Daniel's opinion, the machines weren't getting less common. The recently ramped-up "Drone Purge," as they called the Army's ops, wasn't working.

Even simple degradation and corrosion should have made the machines a rarity by now. But people didn't want to listen to him, especially without proof. He had data to support his claims, but though he'd catalogued every attack report he could get his hands on, it wasn't complete.

Tonight he'd achieve a milestone.

He closed the door and dragged a gun box from under his bed. Out here, everyone knew how to shoot. It wasn't just the drones, after all.

You also had Outmen—people who lived in the wilds and robbed and looted the towns still hanging on to civilization.

Daniel took the lid off the box. The drone limb shone a dull gunmetal gray in the light of his desk lamp.

"You got it from your dad, huh?" he said to himself. Tujo's father dealt in bulk scrap metal recycling. Odds were he'd plucked this piece off one of the military units in the area. They'd long since stopped keeping the parts for research. Tujo would have seen it—he sometimes met his dad at the foundry after school—and must have thought it perfect for his assignment.

Poor Mrs. Suchara. Her youngest daughter had lost an arm to a drone. Tujo should have thought things through. He'd summited Mount Insensitivity bringing a drone component to class.

Daniel put the arm up on his table and worked one of its dangling wires in to a circuit board he'd spent two months soldering. The homemade control module fed a cable to the computer display's small port.

He scrolled to some code of interest on the display. This batch of intelligence files was from a Texas Independent Defense Force server farm he'd hit via several proxies and intrusion methods. Texas was just one of many states talking independence.

He scanned through the lines one more time. He recognized the big blocks of AI subroutines; the algorithms controlling everything from altitude to targeting. They didn't teach this stuff in school, but Daniel had found other ways to learn it. Many guys his age had porn stuffed in their closets; he had old programming books. Something about coding and machine learning had fit into his interests like a keystone.

He found the block of code he wanted, changed some parameters and compiled it.

He took a breath, then, with a keystroke, fed the package to the arm.

The limb straightened, slapping his lamp onto the floor and flattening his notebook against the wall with such force it cracked the drywall behind it. The arm fell off the desk, taking the circuit board with it.

Surprised, Daniel careened backward in his chair, landing on his back under the slowly rotating ceiling fan.

He coughed out, "It works!" Finally! This code, among all the other false leads he'd found, was valid. He could read through it and understand what it was doing.

There was a knock on the door. Daniel was picking himself up as it opened. He'd forgotten to lock it!

"Daniel?" asked his father, entering. He looked at his son, who was scooting his chair back under his desk. The still-rocking, fallen lamp's light swooped in receding arcs off the damaged wall. "Is that what I think it is?"

Daniel frowned.

Franklin Bell was a morose, cautious man, gifted with anything having wires and bolts, and not half bad with software, either, though he didn't share Daniel's passion for the subject. "You got it working, didn't you?"

Daniel put his lamp back on the table. He inhaled, and brushed his bangs out of his eyes. "Tujo didn't want it. I had some code I picked up a while back. I thought I could activate the limb with it."

"I have to admit, I'm impressed you got all this rigged up." He sat down on Daniel's bed. "This is just like you. When you were six, I thought you were playing with toy girders and tin foil in the yard, but you were trying to set up your own radio tower to hear CB signals from the wilds. You, you're always chasing a theory. What is it this time?"

"I don't think the military is making a dent in the drones," said Daniel.

"This again."

"We shouldn't see as many attacks, especially since the Drone Purge started. They should be tapering off."

"The military says there are tens of thousands of drones. They've already destroyed several hundred. Give them time."

"My heat map of attacks and their frequencies would look different if they were right." Daniel wouldn't budge on this point.

"So how does the arm tie into this?"

"Trying to get an understanding of the drone code."

"That's it on your computer, isn't it?"

Daniel nodded.

"You got it off the Internet, didn't you? Somewhere surreptitious?" He smirked at Daniel's expression. "Your dad gave you your intellect, you know."

"It's the only set of files I've seen that looked right, and now I know they work."

His father glanced at the screen. "That's Chinese text."

"Mandarin," said Daniel. "The code is still accessible, though. And I've been picking up Mandarin in my spare time, just in case."

"I bet you have."

Daniel smiled.

"You're too smart to lose," said Franklin. "The drones aren't to be toyed with."

"Once I've reviewed this code, I'll know how to avoid them."

"You already do. Stay inside town, and obey the curfew."

"Dad, I only need to see if they're still popping up nearby. It's basic data gathering, and it will confirm my heat map is not just accurate, but *predictive*. Then I can present my findings."

"No," said Franklin. "That war is still claiming lives, even though we won it. And I won't see you be one of them."

Daniel folded his arms and stared at the code.

"Son, promise me you won't go chasing those things."

"I wasn't talking about *chasing* them."

Franklin waited.

"I promise," said Daniel.

#

School was out for a few days thanks to the 4th of July. Everyone crowded downtown while the ghost of a parade drifted by and off-colored, faded flags were flown. Some of the infantry mustered and marched ahead of an armed transport. They looked tired, and their smiles were forced. Daniel had heard losses were significant, even though the Army had just "surged" in the region.

There were rumors that the states back east were descending further into corruption, squandering resources needed for the Army. Folks—civilian and military alike—felt like shards of ice calving off a glacier, drifting away from the United States into a sea of buzzing machines and wild men.

Daniel feigned wanting to stay home and read. Sandra gave him a hard time about it.

"Great, I've got to meet your buddy Tujo at the fair, and you won't even run interference." But his parents didn't mind much. His mother, Kaitlin, encouraged him to keep at his interests, and in his father's eyes at least he was staying indoors.

#

The town was surrounded by a palisade of concrete blocks. But it didn't run everywhere, and at the drainage area for the neighborhood the palisade gave way to a chain-link fence. A fallen tree had lifted up some of the fence with its trunk, and erosion had dug around the roots, which splayed vertically like the rays of a stylized setting sun. Daniel had to get on his hands and knees, but he was able to squeeze under the fence and between the roots.

And into pure freedom, an irresistible siren that had lured so many out to the frontier, back when the county was young and violent and optimistic all at once.

Daniel was also optimistic. If he was right, he'd have information that would be useful for all those fighting the drones. And he'd been training for this with a series of brief trips taken outside, just to get the lay of the land for his maps.

This time was different, though. He'd be out longer than ever.

He reminded himself what the mostly-complete code had taught him. The drones keyed off movement and noise. But he'd discovered they weren't programmed to acquire targets much above their own altitude. If he could stay to shelves of rock and the sides of hills, and keep hidden, he'd have a good vantage to record their positions and he'd be safe.

He wondered what seeing one would be like.

"Like winning," he whispered to himself.

The wind sighed through the pines, firs, and other hardwoods. Daniel crouched and pulled out a paper topographical map marked with his own notes. He adjusted the shotgun strapped over his shoulder.

There was a rise out and to the left, which overlooked the river. He'd start there.

#

The sun was high, and the river a tumble of diamonds polishing boulders as they went. It wasn't true rapids down there, however, so Daniel could still hear very well. In the shadows, against a cliff wall far above, he had waited for three hours.

He could imagine the splendor of the outdoors as they once were. Before a tyrant had marched armies over the Earth and ravaged so much of it, and dropped his hunter-killer drones all over the

Midwest. Before the alien Nartuni had come and helped mankind defeat the conqueror. That most people didn't know anything about the conflict other than "we owe the aliens a debt" also struck him as not coincidental. One day, he'd learn how it all tied together.

For now, all his generation could do was work with what they knew. All they could do was fight the evil where they saw it.

But as the hours dragged on, he began to second-guess himself. What if he was out here and never saw any drones? And what if the Army and its "Drone Purge," as they called it, eventually *did* clear out the machines? What would he say to everyone else?

He was ruminating on that when there was a shuffling of leaves off to his right.

Daniel focused his gaze on the shrubs and understory trees the disturbance had come from. Perhaps a hundred feet away. So close!

A flash of metal, so brief he wondered if he'd imagined it.

His pulse quickened. He could hear the rush of his own blood in his ears. The river went on, uncaring, and the trees licked the wind with a million tongues, but now Daniel's focus was centered on that patch of green and brown.

His heart thundered. He reminded himself that his position behind the tall grasses along the ledge gave good visibility, and also cover, even if the drone used infrared, which it wouldn't in the day...

Minutes passed. The noise did not come again, nor did the movement. Drones did not stay stationary; everyone knew that. He should have seen it again by now.

He risked rising to his knees. There was nothing on the near side of the river bank, below the ledge. He leaned over more, straining to see the area directly under him, the only blind spot in his entire field of view.

He froze. Six rifle muzzles were pointed upward. At him. For an awful moment, he thought he'd been surprised by Outmen probing the outer reaches of the town for supplies or raiding points while the citizens were distracted.

They weren't Outmen.

#

Okay, so he was dead.

The all-volunteer Civil Militia Patrol was led by Rod Barkley, a coworker of his father's. The idea was they'd make security walks and fill gaps the Army couldn't, while it focused on beating the drones. Sometimes the CMP took down individual drones, but they'd withdraw and call the cavalry if they saw more than they could handle.

Rod marched him home. Like everyone else, he didn't have a mobile phone. They'd been restricted since way back at the end of war, though official justifications didn't make sense. Daniel got to listen to Mr. Barkley's admonishments, spoken around a ball of chewing tobacco, as they walked.

As Daniel and Rod approached the house, a group of off-duty soldiers smoking on the porch asked Rod if he needed anything. Terrific. Not only was Daniel going to be humiliated, it was going to happen in front of the guys who came over to play cards during their R&R time. Daniel was proud his father had served, but in moments like this he wished he'd been an engineer sans the ten years he'd once spent as a technical officer.

Inside, Rod handed him over to Franklin. Franklin excused himself from his card game, apologized to Rod for the "scare in the woods," and then he and Kaitlin walked Daniel to the kitchen.

His father folded his arms as Daniel slinked into a chair. "You enjoy spooking the civil patrol? What if there had been an accident? What would Rod have felt like?"

"Franklin!" Kaitlin, a demure woman most of the time, but loud when she needed to be, added, "What would *we* have felt like?"

"Oh, I'd like to remind our son we love him," said Franklin. "But he clearly doesn't care about that."

"It's because I love you guys that I went out there," said Daniel.

"A few programming books gives you the right to endanger yourself like that?"

"I knew you wouldn't understand."

"You're right. I don't understand why you'd break your word."

"What should I do?" asked Daniel. "When I was five, and supposed to be reading fairy tales, I grew up hearing about Tommy Mushita." Tommy, who'd run into the path of a truck on the highway trying to get away from a drone. "Six kids in middle school, crippled, one that hung himself. Two years ago, Sabrina Martinez loses an arm and a leg but still makes it to the prom a month after, and we're all supposed to stand there and applaud her for being strong. She shouldn't have had to be!"

"You're not going to fix it," said Franklin, softening. "Your heart is in the right place, it's in a Godly place. But those are the facts. That's why the Army is out here."

"They think the drones are being impacted by their operations, and they're not," said Daniel. "Isn't that called bad intelligence?"

"Now that's interesting." An officer in full uniform stood at the door.

"Captain Kurita," said Franklin. "I didn't know you'd come."

"Just got here." Kurita gestured at one of the chairs. Kaitlin indicated it was okay for him to sit. She offered him coffee. He declined.

"I'm glad you could make it," said Franklin.

"Wouldn't miss it," said Kurita. He leaned forward, grinned, and added in a softer voice, "Though I'm mainly here to make sure no one damages an end table again."

Franklin chuckled. "I appreciate that, but it really wasn't a big deal."

"If my men misbehave, it's always a big deal." He eyed Daniel. "I hope I'm not interrupting anything, but I heard what your son was saying. Can I talk to him for a moment?"

"Sure," said Franklin.

Kurita rested his elbows on the table, and spread his hands. "There's no way those drones aren't being dealt a blow, Daniel. We're destroying too many for that not to be the case. Ten this last week alone."

"And how many are left?" asked Daniel.

Kaitlin apologized for her son.

"No, it's okay," said Kurita. "It's true, there's still thousands."

"But your operation should still be having some kind of effect, right?"

Kurita was pleased, until he understood Daniel's meaning. "Why do you think we aren't?"

"My data. I've been monitoring the attacks for two years now. I made a heat map, even—"

"Oh, that's right," said Kurita, waving the concerns away. "Your dad mentioned it recently. See, son, I had to explain to him the incongruence."

Daniel passed a grateful look at his father. So he had considered it, after all.

Kurita leaned forward. "Your theory hinges on the idea that if we're making a dent in the drones, you'd be seeing less of them. But you don't understand how they work. See, we stir them up during combat operations. It's like poking a stick in an ant hill. Did you ever do that as a kid?"

Daniel struggled to remain respectful; he had to remind himself the man was a soldier, risking his life for them all.

Kurita continued: "Yes, you'll see more ants for a while. But that doesn't mean you didn't kill any. Now, I know everyone wants to do what they can to help us, and I appreciate you wanting to do the same. But leave the drones to us."

"Still, if I can get just one drone contact outside of town, it would validate my theory."

"No. Stay inside the palisade and obey the curfew. Next time you cross over, you might not run into a civil patrol. It only takes once."

Daniel gave up. Kurita moved on to small talk with his parents. Daniel did his best to hide his frustration.

What he did not know, at that time, was others had listened to the conversation. Two doors down, his sister had heard it from her room. She knew Daniel would try again, even as Franklin told him he was grounded for three weeks. And back in the living room, pretending to be wrapped up in a card game and inebriated, listened another officer.

But his ears were keen in a way no ordinary man's were.

#

A month later, Daniel was in the garage working on one of his bicycles. He was trying to keep distracted and stay out of trouble.

He heard shouts and people running. Wiping his hands with a shop rag, he walked out of the garage and saw Tim Martuno, a classmate, hustling along with a group of others.

"Tim!" Daniel yelled. "What is it?"

"Tujo," said Martuno. "It's Tujo!"

#

News spread fast, and the hospital—one of the few operational in the entire Zone—was packed when Daniel arrived. In the ER waiting area, an orderly was trying to calm people down. Half were upper classmen.

Daniel pushed his way through the crowd. He heard someone say

Tujo's mom was on the way. His dad would find out soon, if he hadn't already. Daniel scanned the faces and saw Tim at the front desk, pleading to be let back. Tim and Tujo were close.

"No," said the receptionist. "He's not here yet anyway, and he's going straight to surgery when he arrives."

The words had just left her lips when strobing lights fell across them all. An armored ambulance pulled up outside.

Daniel would never forget what he saw. It was surreal.

Nightmarish.

A gurney, wheeled into the room with EMTs at either side. Orderlies shoving people out of the way to "Make a path! Make a path!" A doctor running up, asking vitals. A nurse grabbing the rails and guiding the gurney toward the waiting OR.

Tujo, on his back. Oxygen mask fastened around his face. Eyes wide, orbs within rolling upward. An IV fluid bag dangling from a rack off his shoulder, like a jellyfish pulled from the ocean.

Wrapped stumps where his legs once were.

#

A short time later, one of the nurses came out to tell everyone Tujo had stabilized. She implored them all to go home. Daniel thought this was out of concern for Tujo's parents. What a long, black night lay ahead of them once they got to the hospital.

It wasn't. The staff was expecting more wounded.

"Someone *else* got hit by the drones?" asked Daniel, to the nurse as she turned to leave. "Who?" He braced himself for another mauled neighbor or friend.

"Soldiers," she replied.

#

As he walked home, Army vehicles passed. Tan-colored hulks, they bristled with guns and carried red crosses on a field of white upon their sides—atypical for medical vehicles, but the drones didn't pay attention to the Geneva Convention.

Men and women moaned and begged for help from inside the trucks and transports. Captain Kurita rode in the cab of one truck. He wasn't looking outside and his face was tight with worry. Daniel could have shot off a flare and the man wouldn't have noticed.

But one of the officers, in another, did glance his way. Daniel had seen him before, he thought. Perhaps at his father's card games?

The vehicles passed. The glow of tail lamps faded, leaving only a young man alone in the dark.

Daniel clenched his fists.

He was sure of what he needed to do.

#

He would have to cross through a marshy lowland—more like a muddy field. But on the other side was a hill. People said it'd been fought over during the war. It was supposed to be covered in the remains of impact craters.

If he could make it there, he'd have a commanding view of the area, and nothing would find him. He'd depart where he'd snuck out last time. It was still the best spot; away from the departure point the Army had taken for a major thrust just a day before. Where their stick had stirred up the ants to deadly effect.

According to his dad, one of the Army's recon teams had gotten jumped by five drones. They'd called in help, but by then more drones had appeared...

More evidence, if only he could get someone to see it.

Daniel was back before curfew the Friday night before he'd leave, so no one would suspect him of anything, or notice he'd been gone long enough to stash a bag of supplies at the entry point. He planned to stay on the hill for forty eight hours. He knew they'd be worried when they woke, so he'd leave a note in the kitchen, explaining everything.

But he'd forgotten about Sandra. She lay in bed that night, suspicious. She was sure he was getting ready to do something foolhardy. She kept listening for the door to his room, down the hallway.

At five in the morning, she heard it open. She told herself he probably had a girlfriend. Dad preached waiting until after marriage, but that was hard to do, especially when you saw things like what happened to Tujo. She'd visited Tujo in the hospital, but had been in tears by the time she'd come home.

People needed to stay safe. So if she followed Daniel just to make sure he was, she'd call herself a good sister, not a nosy one.

She stepped out of bed and flew into clothes she'd already placed on the bench.

#

Daniel retrieved his ditty bag from under some leaves and branches where he'd left it. What would his father have done if someone had found the bag already and told him? Ground his son until he was thirty? He might still do that after this, but at least, thought Daniel, he'd have his proof.

And maybe save some lives.

The fence had been re-anchored with concrete post supports. This meant he had to deal with its contact sensors. If he cut the chain-link, he'd set off an alarm.

Luckily, a soldering gun and old electrical wire had provided the solution. He'd spent the prior week visiting the fence and rerouting its links in key areas, just so he'd be ready for this moment.

He took a pair of wire cutters from his bag, and glanced around once more. He clamped the first now-inactive link between the cutters, took a breath, and squeezed.

He startled when the link snapped. But the speakers mounted in the fence posts remained silent.

Fifteen minutes of cutting passed, and soon the coming sun announced itself with trace rose petal pink along the eastern horizon. Daniel was sweating from effort, but his passage was ready.

He crawled through the hole, dragging his ditty bag behind him.

Then he was on the other side once more.

He threaded through the woods, moving northwest. Another two months and the additional cover provided by the deciduous trees would be gone. The summer bugs were worth it.

Daniel had always wanted to go camping, *real* camping, the kind where you didn't have to worry about decades-old drones cutting your limbs off. In the books he'd read on the outdoors, there were always two rules that stood out: One should avoid going alone. And they should always let someone who wasn't going know exactly where they'd be.

He'd broken both. His parents wouldn't have his exact location. Even if they sicced a tracker on him, it'd take them hours to find him. Daniel had read survival books and had practiced hiding his path. He wouldn't be an easy mark. Evasion was just like coding. Cryptic when you first encountered it, then, after a while, second nature.

After an hour, the tree line gave way to the expected marsh. The hill beyond beckoned, lit up in the sun like the distant mountains.

He put a boot in the muck. This was when he was going to be most vulnerable, and the noisiest, so there was no time to delay.

Another step. Water, squeezed from the mud, rose around his boot. But it didn't come higher than his toes, and he was still able to move forward.

Halfway across, it was only up to his ankles.

Before he knew it, he was coming uphill, dark, wet dirt flaking off his boots like animal feces.

The mount was like a giant turtle shell, he decided, pockmarked and pitted, damaged by the battle that once raged over it.

The said the drones had been deployed first, then the long-dead would-be conqueror of Earth had airdropped his own troops right into the same Midwest he'd weakened. The battles were ferocious.

Daniel imagined troops surging up the hill, only to be beaten back, while artillery fire rained around them and the machines stalked both sides, plucking victims from the outskirts of the battle lines.

He felt an urgent pull to return home. He could be back in hours. Safe in his room. In deep trouble, yes, but alive and with his limbs intact.

And he'd be a coward.

He resumed his hike. At the top of the hill, he found a two-foot deep depression and spread a tarp, flattening the tall grass. He put up a second, camo-colored tarp over his head, supporting it with rods staked to the ground with a rubber mallet, so he'd make less noise. What he assembled was almost like a deer blind from back when people hunted.

He clicked the safety off his shotgun and laid it to his right. He took out his notepad, a screw-topped soda, and a pair of polarized binoculars.

Sipping with one hand, he panned the binoculars across the marsh, the woods, the mountains. And saw something. Something unmistakable.

He struggled to believe what was before him.

The figure stood down at the edge of the marsh. Denim. A jacket. Hiking boots.

Sandra. She'd followed him.

Anger boiled inside Daniel, but it was quickly replaced by another emotion—cold, stifling dread. Sandra didn't know the things he did. She was a sitting duck out there. She must have lost him in the woods, because she wasn't looking at him, but everywhere. She started to walk the edge of the marsh.

Breaking his cover was very dangerous, but if Daniel didn't do something, she'd get herself lost, or hurt.

He cursed, grabbed his shotgun, and tore out of cover, rushing down the slope. Small rocks tumbled from his boot steps. He wanted to call out, but that would have been beyond dumb.

Sandra didn't notice him. She reached a point, and turned even further away. Daniel plodded across the marsh, feet slopping and sloshing in a part he hadn't intended to go through, where it was wetter.

Up ahead, Sandra turned to the left and her cheek caught the sun. She was hopelessly exposed. Only luck was keeping them alive. The heat map and the data demanded a drone appear. Mathematically, they were engaging in Russian Roulette with multiple spins every minute, and only two players to take the bullets.

She turned once more and finally saw him. Her shoulders relaxed. Her head lowered in relief.

He stabbed a finger toward the tree line; she shrugged to indicate she didn't understand. Instead, she moved back along the edge of the muck toward a stand of reeds and a sunken boulder. That wasn't as good as the trees, he thought, but it was better than nothing.

The water around his boots was getting more shallow. His nerves were blown, and he was frustrated. Defeat washed over him, cold as a winter morning. His chance was gone. He had to take Sandra home. She might be his annoying older sister, but she'd been worried about his safety, and he needed to honor that, as well as keep her from being killed.

Almost to each other, she risked speaking. "Man, you're royally sliced when we get back. But I'm glad to see you."

"You ruined my work," he said, huffing toward her.

"You're welcome."

He checked to his left and right to make sure they were still clear. There was still nothing. "You shouldn't have done..."

He froze. He felt a rumble in the soil.

She looked at his eyes, blaring with sudden worry. A drone?

No. This was in the *ground*. Like a heavy vehicle approaching. The Army, possibly. But out here, it could also be Outmen. They were

104 JONATHAN C GILLESPIE

known to steal trucks and such.

He'd abandon his gear and they'd run for it. Daniel rushed at her, stepped over the boulder...

And it came out of the ground, shedding mud and dirt. Daniel was thrown forward, landing at his sister's feet.

The marsh bled off the surface of a metal sphere. A cluster of green optical sensors glowed in its center. Water vapor sputtered away from the drone's dorsal side, away from the drive system's heat exchanger as an internal hover-engine spun up to full power.

Daniel and Sandra stumbled backward in terror. But Daniel saw how old the drone was. If they were lucky it might be disarmed or ineffective.

Hope rose as he examined it. It should have had three weapons arms, but one was missing. From the first, an arc torch tried to ignite, but flickered in impotence with tiny blue sparks.

Yes! He believed, for a fraction of a second, that the old machine was harmless.

But then he saw the drone's other arm. A circular blade tipped with tiny saw teeth began spinning at the end of it, faster, and faster. Steam rose from the weapon as it superheated.

The drone charged. Daniel raised his arms and yelped. But the machine had not targeted him.

It fell upon Sandra.

Everything else was a blur, the kind of trauma the brain would have trouble recalling, because it does not want such a specter to darken its rooms.

Daniel recalled only a few things: Sandra screaming. Her severed arm, flying upward, arcing in the midday sun with a red streamer from the end, like a kite with a cut string. The sparks of buckshot on the drone's body as he shot it, to no effect. Him leaping atop the machine, desperate to stop the attack.

Afterward, lying there, unable to pull himself over to comfort her, to tell her she wouldn't die. Because his legs were gone, and he had but one arm left himself.

One hand to wipe his own tears away.

#

The Army had been canvassing the hills looking for them, and ironically was only half a mile away when the attack happened.

On the way into the hospital, Daniel felt nothing. Shock, the medics mentioned. He was hooked up to an IV, but when he came in through the doors on a gurney, and back to the OR, he overheard the doc saying he shouldn't need much blood. The drones always made flash-cauterized, sealed cuts.

To cripple was in their programming, he bitterly recalled. Not to kill.

They put Daniel and Sandra in the same room. Franklin came that night, and held it together while he visited, but Daniel could hear him weeping in the hall. Kaitlin broke down when she saw them. "My babies! My BABIES!" They had to help her out of the ward.

He would never forget the guilt. The next morning, through tears, his father told him the drone was one of two destroyed that day. Daniel asked where the other had been.

Two miles away. Right where it would have made sense.

He had his missing data points.

#

Six years later, Daniel sat in rehab room nine of his children's clinic, a state of the art facility in Boston. Had one not known his past, they would have assumed he was like anyone else, though very rich. His new limbs were based on Nartuni designs, with a few of his own enhancements. Cybernetics were just one of the industries Ascension, his company, was involved in. The aliens hadn't shared all their technology with mankind, but their outpouring of medical guidance was changing lives everywhere, and Daniel was one of those at the forefront.

He watched as a limb moved back and forth, back and forth. Walking up its motion with his eyes, he smiled at the fourteen-year-old girl who'd received it. Patty was a smart kid, and tough. She'd lost an arm in a drone attack, out in what used to be Oklahoma, but she'd finally come up on the list after waiting a year.

"How is it?" he asked.

"It feels different," she said. "But it's... it's..." Her eyes were watering. She was cradling a ball in her new fingertips. With their false skin, they appeared real.

Patty reminded him of his sister, at least as he remembered her. He and Sandra had not spoken in two years. Dad said she'd gotten into drugs after things with Tujo had fallen apart. No one blamed Tujo for leaving. Trauma had brought them together, but where Tujo had recovered from his, Sandra had spiraled downward.

He wondered if she'd ever forgive him, or herself.

"Mr. Bell?" came a voice to his left.

Daniel glanced to his side, and was taken back in time.

The man had once worn a uniform, but today it was an impeccable suit and tie. He had gray around his temples. This was the same officer who'd served in Captain Kurita's unit. Seeing him brought Daniel back to that awful night Tujo and the soldiers had been attacked. And Daniel recalled the officer having been in Kurita's entourage when the captain—morose and worn down—had eventually visited him in the hospital.

"You're not Army," said Daniel. "You're something else."

The words evoked just a trace of surprise on the man's face. He smiled, but it was too satisfied to call it warm. "Command knows you're perceptive, Mr. Bell. As I have known from my first encounter with you."

"Command?" He raised an eyebrow. "Who's Command?"

The little girl had wandered off with one of the trainers she liked.

The man avoided the question. "What if I told you there was a way to ensure your clinic would have all the Nartuni limbs it would ever need? That you could rehabilitate hundreds, and not simply—how many has it been so far?"

"Forty-eight," said Daniel. *And a waiting list a thousand deep.*

"The fact of the matter is your data matches our own. We don't know why the drones haven't dropped in number. Command has watched your work with Ascension, and we believe you'd be valuable help with some special projects."

"Who are you?"

"This is your sole chance, Mr. Bell. I have answers, but they won't be delivered here. You have your afternoon clear, do you not?"

"How did you know that?"

"Yes or no. Will you come with me?"

"All the limbs we need?"

"All."

Out in the parking lot waited a spotless, blacked-out car. Daniel climbed inside and the soldier sat next to him. The gullwing doors hissed shut.

"I'm pleased you're interested," said the officer. "People who can see problems from a different perspective are valuable to us."

"And where's your particular vantage point?" asked Daniel.
"In orbit."

-o-

Jonathan C. Gillespie has been writing fiction for nearly twenty years. His work has been featured in magazines, podcasts, and other venues, and has achieved multiple award nominations, including the Parsecs. "Right Hand" is a prequel to *Revenant Man*, Book One of The Tyrant Strategy, a military science fiction series.

Homepage: **http://jonathancg.net**
Mailing List: **http://eepurl.com/su_xD**

What Make is Your Cat?

by Richard Crawford

The air-tube climbed slowly over the lagoon, a glass worm oozing into the sky. Beneath the rails, Atlantis-London shimmered, an expanse of glassy manmade lagoons, blue water topped by glistening steel and glass towers reaching into the clouds. In contrast, the Tower of London squatted like a toad on its moat-bordered island. St Paul's a ghostly presence pearlescent beneath its sea dome. Water lapped at the rooftops of unsaved buildings, eating the past.

I'm too young to remember what London looked like before the flood. Weird to think, in my granddad's day people went around in tunnels beneath the ground, like moles or worms. I'd never seen real a worm or a mole, only pictures. Most of the animals were lost in the flood; a few mutated into something different, but that's not a good story.

Dad told me about the old London, the view from the Shard: how Granddad proposed to Gran there. He wanted to do the same when he asked Mum to marry him, but he couldn't afford the entrance fee. They were all gone, and the view from the top of the Shard was nothing special now. I looked south to where it rose glittering from the waters, lower levels sealed and submerged. Dwarfed by the new cloud towers.

"What make is your cat?"

It took me a moment to realize the girl was asking me a question. "Huh?"

"Your cat," the girl said, with that special clarity and patience the rich reserved for plebs; not that there are many of us left in Atlantis-London. "What make is it?"

I stared, taking her in properly for the first time. Her head, shaved close to leave only the finest golden stubble, was enough to suggest she was a swimmer. The aqua shorts and tiny breathing apparatus she wore confirmed it. Multihued tattoos covered her arms and breasts; her skin still glittered with drops of water, though it was drying rapidly in the air-conditioned carriage. A pair of gossamer thin, pearly hued flippers lay by her feet.

I realized she must have boarded the air-tube at the Tower Bridge aerostation. I hadn't even noticed a bare breasted swimmer-girl dripping next to me. That's how much things had changed. The old social paradigms and wiring were slowly dying. No point assessing what would never be available. I wondered what Granddad would have made of it.

Not everyone was a swimmer. Extreme swimming began as a new fitness craze; you couldn't jog outdoors in Atlantis-London, and it quickly developed a class status. It was one of the quickest ways to get around Atlantis-London (Londoners hated the name but AtlantisCorp had insisted, after all it was their money that saved the city), and just as London and its buildings had adapted to the flood, swimmers had developed their own fashion conventions, and some said they were evolving physically too.

The Mayor had tried to ban swimmers from going topless, but she'd been fighting a losing battle. Swimmers were the new elite, invariably fit and healthy, mostly rich, often young professionals: the key workers in the money markets, the new royalty, backed by the power of AtlantisC and the other corporations. Money kept the waters out, one way or another. But only for the chosen few. Ninety percent of London and most of the south-east was gone. Despite the years of preparation, no one expected what happened and millions died in the flood.

I realized the swimmer-girl was waiting, impatient, staring at me as if I was an idiot.

"Chausie," I said, and watched the girl's eyes widen. "Pure bred and licensed." It was foolish to boast in public, but her condescension stung my pride; this rich swimmer-girl was out of my league and Celeste my only equity in the game.

"A Chausie," she breathed, and bent closer to get a better look. She pushed her fingers through the bars of the carry cage, and Celeste deigned to have her head stroked. She knew how to charm a potential client.

"What's it called?"

"Celeste."

"A female," the girl exclaimed and leaned even closer, studying Celeste eagerly.

She was so caught up in my cat, she was hardly aware of my presence now, but I was used to that. A silver drop of water trembled on the end of her nipple and slipped to dampen my shirt. The swimmer-girl didn't notice. I tried not to; perhaps the old wiring was live after all.

"Where did *you* get a cat like this?" she asked. The sudden change in manner jarred for a moment. It was a noticeable switch, the charm vanishing, a reminder that Celeste's social status and desirability were high above mine.

I was careful not to look offended or guilty. It wasn't hard to spot that I didn't belong among the elite of Atlantis-London. Celeste was my primary source of income, my ticket to a few feet of dry sleeping space in the city. I knew a swimmer-girl wasn't interested in me.

"I have an owner's certificate." It wasn't an easy admission, tantamount to saying she was right, I wasn't good enough for my cat.

"With you now?" the girl asked.

"Yes," I said quietly, checking out the other passengers to see if anyone was paying too much attention to our conversation. I didn't want to be mugged, for Celeste to be cat-napped.

The swimmer-girl looked at me, her stare hooded. It was obvious that she had assessed and categorized me; mouth-breather, not worth her time. She returned her attention to Celeste.

"Can I see it?"

"Not here." I wasn't that crazy.

"How many litters?"

This girl was crazy. I shook my head, tight-lipped, regretting the urge to show off.

She pouted for a moment. Then she smiled, switching on the effortless charm. "What's your name?"

"Tommy." It came out surly, but I wasn't dumb enough to fall for her smile.

"Come back with me, Tommy."

I wasn't falling for that either. "Only if you can afford her. Where do you live?" I enjoyed the look on her face as the power ebbed my way. She didn't like it, and for a moment, a frown marred her perfect features, but she wanted my cat badly.

"Kensington lagoon."

A good address. Probably not city money, but solid old money and that was nearly as good.

"Celeste has another appointment," I said primly. We knew how to play hard to get.

"I'll pay double." She didn't waste time wooing us with the niceties, or hide the fact that she had summed me up.

Fair enough, down to business. "What breed is your tom?"

"Chausie," she said, sounding nearly as proud as I was, and I warmed to her a little. "But not pure."

Celeste hissed and turned her back on the girl. We both smiled.

I thought about it. She'd pretty much said I could name my price. Celeste was ready for action and, despite the flounce, she wasn't going to care who we went home with.

"What return were you looking for?" I had a template contract in my satchel.

"What are her numbers?"

"Two point five a litter." It was a good survival rate, nowadays.

The girl frowned as she thought about it. "I want an option on the full litter."

"No."

"Seventy-five percent then."

It was steep, but we'd be paid upfront and the risk was on her side, she might get two kittens, she might get one.

I nodded. But this wasn't the place to get into the details. At least one of the other passengers was listening. "We can sort everything out when we get to your flat."

"We'll get off at Harrods water gate, you'll need a boat," she said.

Of course, I would need a boat. Celeste wasn't going to swim, and neither was I. It was a subtle warning and a less than subtle putdown. As if I needed a reminder, swimmers considered non-swimmers a sub species. There were new areas of Atlantis-London accessible only to swimmers.

The news and advertisement feeds were full of it, along with the physical differences developing between swimmers and non-swimmers. There were rumors of clinical trials to develop products to support this new life style, though no-one knew anyone who had volunteered. *The future of the human race was amphibian.* It had started as a joke, but the real joke was that after all the progress, reaching for the stars, we were going back to where we started.

The deal agreed, the swimmer-girl ignored me, tapping at the console on her wrist. I studied her, careful not to be obvious. Long lean muscles, firm skin, possible genetic selection but, for those that could afford it, genetic selection had been common for a while now. She showed signs of some high quality physical enhancement, scars hidden by tattoos and her features just too perfect. The tattoos told some sort of story, if you knew how to read them. I didn't. If she'd been a corporate or a banker, her tats would have shown company affiliation; I could recognize a few of those, but she was old money of some sort and her tats meant nothing to me.

The air-tube slid imperceptibly down to Harrods water gate. The doors hissed open and Kensington lagoon lay in front of us. The gothic splendor of Harrods, floating incongruously behind the gate, cast a heavy shadow.

There was a long queue for the water-taxis. Wealthy tourists visiting Harrods, some things didn't change. The swimmer-girl sighed impatiently.

"Thirty-one, seventy-five, fifteen." She snapped out her address. "Will you remember that?"

I nodded, not pleased to be treated like an idiot. Before I had time to register offence she was gone. A sleek dive and a blur of motion cutting through the ice blue waters.

It took a few minutes for the queue to clear. As it was coming up to my turn there was an altercation between the water-taxi drivers, and a reorganization. I waited impatiently, the taste of money dry in my mouth. The boat that slid gently up to my station was driven by a heavyset man, his tattoos hidden beneath a creased t-shirt. He held the boat steady as we boarded, Celeste now hidden beneath the carry-cover.

"Where you going, mate?"

"Thirty-one, seventy-five, fifteen."

He hardly seemed to wait for my response. The boat purred softly out into the lagoon, keeping to the speed limit and the designated water lanes. I raised a hand to shield my eyes and looked for the girl, but she was far across the lagoon and lost to sight.

Beneath the waters, the mansions of old Kensington crumbled. Around the lagoon, the glass and steel of new Kensington stabbed towards the sky.

It took a while to reach the girl's apartment tower. As we drew close, I stared up and up, the top levels of the tower out of sight among the clouds.

The waterman brought the taxi up against the water-gate with a gentle bump. I was still staring up into the sky and felt a sudden reluctance to take Celeste into the glass and steel palace. Truth was she belonged here more than I did.

I sighed and started to climb ashore.

"Something up, kid?" the waterman asked.

The question made me more uneasy, as if he was suggesting that something was up.

"Will you wait?" Paying him to wait would eat into my profit, but Celeste had other appointments, there were ways to get around the testing.

He shook his head. "Sorry, it's busy today."

Hanging on to Celeste's cage, I climbed ashore and walked to the entrance. When I punched seventy-five fifteen, the girl's face appeared on the screen almost immediately. I had no clue what her name was, but she didn't bother with niceties.

"Take elevator three," she instructed. "It will bring you straight to us."

I didn't like the way she said *us,* but maybe she meant her tomcat.

I peeled the cover back and looked at Celeste. She stared back, lashed her tail a couple of times, and gave a sharp meow, clearly unimpressed.

"You're right," I agreed. "But we can't afford to pass this up."

A chance encounter, it's not as if the girl could have planned this. I was being paranoid, but Atlantis-London did that to you, nothing came easy, and without a lot of money, it was hard to stay safe.

The lift was so fast and smooth we arrived before I noticed any sense of motion. The doors slid open to a wash of brilliant sunlight. I blinked and hesitated. The swimmer-girl was waiting for us; she was wearing nothing more than a sliver of material around her waist, and sunglasses. There was no sign of the tomcat, or any other *us.*

I stepped off the lift and placed Celeste's cage on the floor.

"It's alright to let her out," the girl said. She watched in silence as I released the catch.

Celeste was an old hand at house calls. She emerged slowly, sauntering out of her cage like an empress visiting a conquered nation, but on her guard at the same time. A short walk around the minimalist room and she settled in the sunlight to attend to her grooming.

"She's beautiful," said the girl, her tough exterior slipping for a moment.

We both watched Celeste, a shared moment of admiration. It didn't last. The girl's wrist console beeped discreetly and she snapped back to business.

"I need to see her paperwork and health certificates."

By the time we were done, Celeste had completed her toilet and stretched out in the sun. The swimmer-girl seemed almost nervous and impatient to get on with things. Celeste was happy, so I agreed, and the girl went to get her tomcat. She returned, and Marvin entered behind her. He was a large tom with a swaggering bowlegged walk; Celeste flicked a look over her shoulder and then ignored him. He was a good-looking cat, not in Celeste's league but she would do her duty.

"Best to leave them to get to get to know each other," I said. "I have a template contract." Time for business. Time to make money. I was already spending it in my head. Perhaps there'd be enough for a treat for Celeste and something for me.

"Of course." The swimmer-girl smiled, switching up the charm again. "Would you like something to drink first?"

I was about to refuse when it occurred to me that I was probably passing up a chance to taste real fruit juice. "Yes, please."

One of the latest Butbots appeared as if by magic.

"Whatever you want," said the girl smugly. "Just ask."

Instinct warned me to caution, but I couldn't resist. "Orange juice, please," I said, and held my breath.

The swimmer-girl's lips kinked in a cruel little smile. I couldn't work out if it was my awed juice request or my politeness to the Butbot she found ridiculous.

The little robot wheeled around and returned quickly with a small glass of juice.

I took it reverently. The first mouthful of juice burst on my tongue, chunky and acidic, nothing like the chemical constructs that were all

I could afford. Any sort of fresh food was way beyond my means.

After the first mouthful, I swallowed greedily, sucking the last shreds of pulp from the empty glass. Hopeful of another, I looked for the girl, but she had followed Celeste and Marvin. Again, as if by magic, the Butbot appeared offering another glass of juice.

"Thank you," I said, fixated by its gently contoured face.

I could hear Celeste and Marvin exchanging insults. I wanted to tell the girl to leave them alone, but this was her apartment and it's always best to keep the client sweet until you've been paid. I sucked down the glass of juice and stared at the Butbot's sad face, wondering what it had seen and heard.

I sensed movement and looked up, somewhat embarrassed to be caught mooning over a house robot.

It was not the swimmer-girl.

The man had dark satiny skin with pale ghostly tattoos. He was tall, maybe six-eight, or nine. Head shaved, a pale scar running across his scalp. A swimmer. Seeing him, I took an instinctive step backwards. I realized he must have been in the flat the whole time. That was a bit weird. The girl came to stand beside him, very close but not touching.

"What's his name?" the man asked. He was staring at me.

"Tommy," said the swimmer-girl in the same tone she would have used to introduce Celeste or Marvin.

I felt strange, as if I was shrinking under their gaze. The Butbot rolled silently away from me.

"Celessst," I tried to call, but my tongue was numb. I swallowed but it didn't help. When I took a step, my knees folded. I reached for a chair, but my hand missed and pawed empty air. "Wha…" The orange juice, I realized, with a terrible sinking feeling.

A moment later, I was face down on the polished wood floor. Panic rippled over me. They were going to steal Celeste. A shadow blocked the sun as the man came closer.

"We have a pick up," he was speaking to a microphone on his wrist console. His voice was rich and cultured, but the tone was hard as a hustler's.

"What do you have for me?" a disembodied voice responded.

They were going to steal Celeste. They already had a buyer. I tried to move and only managed to wriggle like a landed fish.

"Male, early twenties," said the man, looking down at me dispassionately. "Yes, healthy enough for early phase research trials." He paused to listen. "Yes, I'd say fit enough for experimental devices."

It took a moment for my fogged brain to realize he wasn't talking about Celeste, another moment to understand what he was talking about and for real panic to set in. I tried to move and flopped helplessly. The girl laughed.

"Usual arrangement," said the man. "We'll take any leftovers."

I couldn't move a muscle. From my worm's eye view, I watched Celeste saunter into the room. She walked over to me and sat down. I stared into her golden eyes.

Celeste licked her lips.

-o-

Richard Crawford writes horror (ghost stories) and epic fantasy. He is the author of the novels Ghost House, Ghost Town and Ghost Mate (The Soul Mate series) and the Traitor Blade Books 1-3, (epic/historical fantasy and recent semi-finalist in the Self Published Blog for fantasy books). His new book, Ghost Road will be released in early 2017.

Homepage:
https://richardcrawfordauthor.com
Mailing list:
https://richardcrawfordauthor.com/contactmail-list

Kaxian Duty

by Cherise Kelley

My tail went under my belly and wagged as fast as it could while Dad prepared me one more time by the backyard fence.

"Check the scent messages before you turn." He turned his head sideways and looked at me.

"Yes, Dad." I rolled over on my back to show him I knew he was boss.

He licked my belly, which made me laugh and roll around on my back because it tickled, and then Dad raised his nose to tell me I should get up. "You'll find Kaxian Headquarters with no problem, if you follow the scent messages."

"I'll follow them, Dad."

I was concentrating hard, so my tail didn't go under my belly. I was able to keep its wag down to a slower rate than a minute ago, but it was still going pretty fast. I've always hated that part of being a puppy: not being able to control my tail. It told everyone exactly what I was thinking!

Not remembering my past lives is a close second on my list of reasons I hate puppy-hood. All the grown-ups said the memories from my past lives would come back to me as I got older. I wanted to believe them, but until it happened, I had to take their word for it, which made me feel dependent on them. I didn't like that.

I've loved every set of parents I ever had, though. This life, my dad is a calm German Shepherd. He pulled the skin back from his teeth and smiled at my wagging tail. "You'll be fine, Clem. Remember, it's the first day for all the other puppies, too. They'll be just as nervous as you are."

Clumsy with my muscle control, I tried a few times before I managed to smile back at him.

Kax! I hate being a puppy!

"You think so?"

Dad amazed me by acting young all of a sudden. He jumped around and wagged his own tail widely. "I know so. I was a puppy once, you know."

I sat down and scratched under my collar with my hind foot.

Dad stopped jumping around, sat down in front of me, and lowered his head so that we saw eye to eye.

I tried to make him understand my situation. "My head knows you were a puppy once, but only because you've told me so. The memories still aren't coming to me."

Dad licked my face a few times. "One thing at a time, Son. You want to be a defender, right?"

All by itself, my tail wagged widely. I didn't mind too much, because that made Dad smile.

He nuzzled my neck and spoke in a soothing tone the words that later on, I wished I had heeded. "Yeah! You want to be a defender, so hurry and get to your first day of Kaxian Duty on time today. Do your best at that. Worry about the memories another day."

Third on my list of things to hate about being a puppy is the short attention span. Clarity of purpose is not my strong point, but we'll get to that in a minute. Dad was there right then. Sigh. I closed my eyes and snuggled against Dad for a moment.

He nosed me until I opened my eyes. "Remember, if you get into danger, call on Kax for help. If the Niques bother you, just run."

I panted to show I understood. "I'll remember."

Dad smiled at me again, and then slapped his front paws down.

I slapped mine down to match, as he'd taught me, even though I knew by the way his tail was wagging slowly that he wasn't going to attack.

Dad's voice came out fast and loud as he noted the time by the lay of the sun's rays. They were peeking up from behind Headquarters Mountain. "OK! Go ahead! Dig your hole and get going, off to duty. You can tell us all about it when you get home."

Mom had come to see me off, too. They both licked my head once to tell me, "Kax be with you."

They blocked the view from their human's den while I dug under the fence.

Looking back once to see Mom and Dad wagging their tails goodbye to me, her Queensland Heeler body slightly smaller than his, I ran down the dirt-and-gravel alley toward the first scent post.

Wow, I'm out of the yard!

An orange and white cat's eyes glowed from the shadow of a cinder-block wall. When she knew that I'd noticed her, she put her ears back. Her tail whipped the ground once before she leaped up on top of the wall, hissed at me, and snarled out insults. "Go home to your moldy old planet, you filthy alien!"

She had insulted Kax! I looked around for a way to get up there. Seeing where the ground sloped up a bit at the end of the wall, I ran over and up on top of the wall.

She jumped down then, of course.

I ran back to the slope and down into the alley again, and then the chase was on!

I was gaining on her!

I was going to get her!

But then she turned toward the street.

I started to turn after her. That's when an odd thing happened.

One second, I was chasing the cat with complete abandon, angrier than I'd ever been in my life—all three months of it. The next second, the first scent post appeared in my mind. A second after that, Dad's voice sounded in my memory. "Check the scent messages before you turn."

I shook my head, and that led to shaking my whole body. Yeah, yeah. It wasn't very big when I was three months old. I know.

I gave up on the cat. I needed to get to Headquarters early so I would get to be a defender. Proud of making the right decision, I went to sniff the first scent post, a telephone pole. It told me to turn right. I left my own scent message so others would know I was on my way, and then I turned right.

I was running down the sidewalk, minding my own business, when two Niques saw me from behind their pristine white picket fence.

They were grown-up Chihuahuas, but they both stuck their tongues out at me and crossed their eyes! And then, on their tiny little legs, they ran to the door of their human's den, scratched at it, and called out.

"Humans!"

"A Kaxian's loose outside!"

"Call the dog catcher!""

"Catch this Kaxian yourself!"

"Take him to the animal shelter!"

"He's dangerous!"

"He's going to hurt us, Humans!"

"Help!"

The Niques are such liars! Those two made me mad, even though I knew their humans would just hear a noise like wolves barking.

Humans can't understand us aliens. They call us dogs, and even the Niques go along with that. It's the one thing Kaxians and Niques agree on: No humans can know that dogs are aliens.

We weren't agreeing on anything right then. These two annoying Niques were still telling lies about me!

"This Kaxian is a known thug, Humans!"

"He comes around here every day, trying to hurt us!"

"Help us, Humans!"

"Open the door!"

"Come out and get him!"

I was running up and down their fence, searching for the best place to get through it, over it, or under it.

"You'll be yelling, 'Help!' with a different tone when I get in there!"

I couldn't wait to make them stop telling lies about me. They were smaller than me even when I was only three months old.

But that odd thing happened again. The sight of the next scent post came into my mind. A second later, Dad's voice came into my memory again. "If you have trouble with the Niques, then just run."

Heeding my memory of Dad, I just ran on by those two lying Niques in their yard. My heart beat extra fast for the next mile or so, until I figured no human could catch up to me. Then my heart slowed to normal speed.

I did well after those two distractions. I didn't chase the squirrels in the park. I didn't tip over the garbage can that smelled like French fry crumbs. I understood what was going on. Somehow, Kax was making sure I got to Headquarters on my first day of duty.

The scent trail led me first up into the barren hills outside the town, and then deep down into a cave.

Yeah, the cave was dark, but that didn't scare me. It only smelled like Kaxians down there. Half way down, I could hear Kaxians talking, more Kaxians than I had ever seen in my whole three months of life. Yeah, I know that's not long. Anyway, I recognized some of their voices. We Kaxians talk to each other across great distances, and I had heard them from home.

At the bottom of the cave, I stopped at a metal door and heard a computerized voice. "Identify."

Of course, if humans went down there with flashlights, they would just see rocks and hear a wolf barking. The metal door is well-disguised.

Glad now that Dad had explained all this to me over and over, I put my front paws up on two metal rocks and held my eyes open while the computer scanned me and verified that no non-Kaxians were with me.

The metal door opened soundlessly to a dark room, and I went inside. The light came on once the door had closed, and another door opened into a wide chamber that smelled of plastic and more metal.

Dad was right. There were many other puppies there, some a month older than me, but some a month younger. All of their tails were wagging quickly under their bellies while the grown-up Kaxian instructors looked them over.

There were Rottweilers, Irish Setters, Great Danes, and many others that the humans call "large breed dogs." There were no "small breed dogs" present. Those are the Niques, our arch rivals. We would never let them into our headquarters. But who cares about the Niques, anyway?

One of the instructors looked me over. All by itself, my tail went under my belly again and started wagging quickly. The instructor nosed me toward a group of puppies, so I wedged myself in between a black Labrador and an American Bulldog. As soon as the instructor went away, we started talking in hushed tones.

"Hi, I'm Clem."

The bulldog pulled his big belly off the floor and turned to me. "I'm Lido."

The black Labrador shook herself and smiled at us. "I'm Skil!"

All three of our tails came out from under us and wagged more slowly as we stood there grinning at each other. We talked for a minute about how old we were and which Kaxian stories we liked the best, and then Lido lay down on his big belly again.

Following Lido's eyes, I turned around and saw the instructor coming back. My tail went back under my belly and did the telltale quick wag once more. So did Skil's.

I whispered to Lido, "Now I see why you lie down on your belly!"

He grinned at me.

Skil warned us, "Shh! He's coming!"

Our instructor was a Mastiff. For sure, he heard us whispering. We Kaxians can hear deer running a mile away. We can hear everything you say no matter how many rooms are between us in the house. So yeah, he heard us. He didn't say anything about it, though. He spoke not only to the three of us, but to the larger group we were in, about twenty puppies in all.

"I'm Koog, your Kaxian duty instructor. All of you, say, 'Hello, Koog.'"

"Hello, Koog."

"Now, I know you're very curious what your duty will be."

All of our mouths opened, and our tongues came out so that we panted. I was too excited to be embarrassed, though.

This is it! Come on, say we're defenders!

"I will be teaching you how to mine jex, starting tomorrow."

I guess my tail gave me away again.

Lido said, "Aw, cheer up, Clem. We don't have to stay miners forever. You can earn a promotion."

"Yeah, I know. I was hoping to be a defender, though," I said.

Skil said, "I met you guys, and that makes me happy."

We both grinned at her, and then at each other.

Koog spent the rest of the day explaining where we would mine tomorrow, how we would know the way there, and how to mine for jex. Just before we left for the day, we met the defenders.

"Hi, I'm Heg."

Together, all of us miners said, "Hi, Heg."

"These are the puppies I'll be training as scouts for our team."

I looked the new scouts over, sure that I would find some physical aspect they all shared which would qualify them as scout defenders. I couldn't see even one. Some of them were bigger than all the miners, sure, but some were smaller. Some were long-legged runners like me, but others were barrel-chested fighters like Lido.

As usual, an introduction meant familiarizing ourselves with each other so we could put a name with a scent. This took a while because with the defenders, there were forty puppies in our new pack, and Heg had also brought two adult miners and four adult defenders. Finally, it was time to go home for the night.

After the new scouts were excused first, Heg addressed the miners.

"I'm sure you all wonder why you weren't chosen to be defenders."

There our tails went again, giving away our anxiety with their frantic wagging underneath our bellies. To make it worse, all our mouths opened, too, and we all panted loudly.

"It's simple. The first twenty to arrive became defenders."

Our tails stopped wagging. Some of our ears went down. No one was stupid enough to say it out loud, but Heg could tell he'd made us mad.

"I can see you think that's not fair."

Kax! There our tails went again, back under our bellies and wagging quickly! Skil rolled over onto her back to show Heg she knew he was boss. Slowly, one by one, we all copied her.

Heg raised his nose in the air, telling us to get up. We did. He went on.

"Obedience is the most important quality in a defender. The first twenty obeyed the order to get here on time. See you all tomorrow! On time!"

Lido, Skil and I worked out our route home so we could run together the farthest before any of us had to turn away toward our own den.

Those two Niques behind their pristine white picket fence started with the lies.

"Humans!"

"A pack of unruly Kaxians is here!"

"They're invading your den!"

I opened my mouth to tell them to quit, but Lido nosed me in the shoulder and started running. He ran as best he could with his big belly, anyway.

Realizing he was right because Dad had told me to just run if the Niques bothered me, I ran right past the Niques, too. So did Skil.

When we were well past them, we all stopped and grinned at each other, wagging our tails slowly behind us.

My den was the first we came to. Mom and Dad were waiting by my hole under the fence, to hear all about my day. I was surprised to realize I was a little sad that Lido and Skil had to go on home to their own dens. I focused on the good part.

"See you tomorrow!" I told both my new friends.

"On time!" we all said together.

Why had I been so nervous? I told Mom and Dad that all in all, my first day of Kaxian duty had been pretty sweet.

-o-

Cherise Kelley wrote this story and three related novels when she could no longer ignore her brain's musings that her dog was not just a pet, but something more extraordinary.

Homepage: **http://www.dogaliens.com**

Lessons Learned

by J Naomi Ay

Although I had known since practically my first memory that I was destined for a career in Spaceforce, and hopefully, a future captaincy of a starship, I had to admit, the prospect of actually going to the Academy was pretty daunting.

"Easy peasey," my grandmother, Captain Jill, said. "I still remember exactly how it was when I was a cadet. The worst part was having to wake up at 0500 every morning. Everything else was a slam dunk, no problem at all. You'll do awesome, Ary. You're just like me."

My grandfather, Captain Lance, snorted from his recliner across the room. He was watching a football game, a beer and a slice of pizza in his hands. "Talk about pretentious snobs," he muttered, waving his pizza at the vid and the game. "In my experience, everyone who went to the Academy was an ass."

Grandma Jill rolled her eyes and made a similar snorting noise in her nose, while I glanced at Kit, my step-sister and fellow future cadet. She also rolled her eyes and shook her head, only slightly, just enough for me alone to see.

"Since Ary's already a pretentious snob, he'll fit right in," Kit announced, never one to hold back on her true opinions. Normally, I would have assumed my step-sister was joking, in which case there ought to have been a twinkle in her bright blue eyes. Instead, they looked hard and her mouth was a thin straight line.

"Thanks, Kit." I smiled a little, still hoping she was teasing. I wasn't a pretentious snob, was I? Certainly, I didn't try to be. Frankly, most of the time I just kept my mouth shut and my opinions to myself. If that came across as snobbish, it wasn't my fault.

Kit sniffed loudly and turned away, dragging a hand through her curly blue hair, while shaking her head again as if I was too stupid to figure it out. Since, we had both turned sixteen, Kit had been experiencing a midlife crisis of sorts. No matter what I did, or how I did it, I was wrong. My step-father Kyle, was in the same boat. She snapped at him just as much, if not more than me. He didn't dare open his mouth when we were home, else Kit, or my mom, Sandy, might bite off his head.

Sometimes, Kyle would glance at me when this was happening, when one or the other was throwing a fit over something stupid like finding the toilet seat left up. "PMS," he'd mouth, raising an eyebrow conspiratorially, or punching me in the arm.

I'd nod back and shrug a little, as if to say, "Yep, Kyle. It's us versus them."

Kyle liked this. It made him happy that we were buddies. I liked making people happy, especially when it was as simple as this to do. Sometimes, I wished I could make Kit happy again, but apparently, that was way beyond my control.

"Asshole!" Grandpa Lance shouted, and for a moment I thought he was referring to me, to my pretentiousness and my snobbiness, of which Kit was such an authority. "Who did he think he was throwing to? The only guys down the field are the opposing team. What a jerk. Jill, will you get me another beer?"

"What's wrong with your legs?" my grandmother snapped. "Are they not working again or is the kitchen too far away?"

At this point, Kit inclined her head slightly towards the door, which was my signal that it was time for us to leave. At nearly two thousand square feet, with an upstairs, a downstairs, and a bedroom for everyone, my grandparents' condo was practically a mansion compared to our usual haunting ground of a tiny cabin aboard a starship. Except when my grandparents started fighting. Then, the condo felt as claustrophobic as a closet. No matter where we went in the house, we could still hear Jill bitching at Lance, or Lance snapping at Jill, or both of them yelling for no apparent reason.

"Where are you going?" Jill demanded, as I jumped up and headed to the door.

"We're going for a walk," Kit replied, already on the front steps.

"It's still a hundred and fifteen out there."

"It's alright, Jill. They're young and can handle the heat. Idiot! There he goes again. He might as well throw it backwards for all the good he's doing. Bench him! I tell you, that coach is as much a dummy as his player. By the way, will you turn the air conditioning up?"

"It's freezing in here. I'm not moving it a single degree. If you're hot, go back to outer space."

"I might, just to get away from you. In the meantime, I'm going to watch the game in my underwear." My grandfather stood up and immediately pulled down his trousers.

"Lance, looking at you is making me ill."

"Jill, I am long past sick when it comes to looking at you."

At this point, I shut the door, racing down the front steps in pursuit of Kit and her blue pony tail. For some odd reason, I always liked to walk behind Kit, to watch that rope of curly blue tresses bounce up and down. When I was little, I liked to yank it and make her scream. Of course, I wouldn't dream of doing that now, not if I wanted to retain any of my limbs.

"Hey! Wait up," I called instead, the heat blasting like a furnace in my face.

Even though the sun was almost completely set, it really was still about a hundred fifteen degrees. Frankly, I hated this kind of weather. Actually, I hated weather of any kind, having spent most of my life almost completely in outer space.

Since my mom was captain of the S/S Asteroid, and Kit's dad was the executive officer, both my step-sister and I only rarely set our feet on solid ground. Usually, it was during the brief periods when the Asteroid went on missions in the dark, or when Spaceforce decided it was too unsafe to have civilian family members aboard. Then, Lance and Jill would pack us up, and take us off to Disneyplanet, or a beach. Usually, this was followed by an extended stay here at the condo north of Tucson.

"Just think, Ary," Kit sighed, her pace slowing a little, the disdain gone from her voice, replaced by something else. "In two more years, we won't have to come here. We can stay in the dorms at school. That's what I'm going to do. I don't care if it's a holiday or midterm break. I'm going to tell my dad I've got to study, and I can't leave."

"Yeah, me too," I said, even though I didn't necessarily agree. It was just easier to let Kit think we were on the same page.

"I'm never going back to outer space, or back here to this sandpit, Arizona," Kit continued, reaching into her pocket and casually lighting herself a cigarette. She waved it at me, offering it, even though she knew I didn't smoke. I didn't like it, and I didn't want to get in trouble with my mom.

Once, when we were aboard the Asteroid, I had taken a puff of one of Kit's cigs, and five minutes later, my mom smelled it on my breath.

"Don't you start smoking!" she scolded, and then hissed something about how I was turning out just like my father, whose tobacco addiction was just one of his many vices.

My father, incidentally, was a *persona non grata* when it came to my mother, my grandparents, and just about everyone else. We didn't talk about him. We didn't think about him. We didn't acknowledge he existed, although sometimes, especially at night when I couldn't sleep, I would pretend to text him.

Even thought it was a stupid thing to do, one worthy of someone six, and not sixteen, I'd pull out my cell and write him a message, just telling him about my life. Of course, I never really sent it, and so I didn't get an answer. Probably, he wouldn't have answered anyway. He was far too busy.

"What do you mean you're never going back to space?" I asked, now strolling beside Kit as the sun sunk low on the desert horizon. It was inexorably hot, but the sky was a beautiful mix of red and orange colors, which almost made it worth being outside. "What's the point of going to the Spaceforce Academy if you don't intend to serve on a starship?"

"No point," Kit agreed, breathing out a gust of smoky gray air. "I'm not going to the Academy." Turning to me, she grabbed one of my hands. "I'm not joining Spaceforce, Ary. I'm going to do something else instead."

I was totally stunned. Those four words, *I'm not joining Spaceforce,* flipped my world upside down. For a moment, I couldn't speak, which might have been a good thing as undoubtedly, I would have said something that sent Kit into a rage.

Kit was supposed to go to the Academy, just like me. Since we were infants, we had been raised on the S/S Asteroid, sharing the same crib, and everything else. We had spent practically every day together, and nights too when we were young. We were like twins except for the fact that she was short, blue haired, and partially Andorian, while I was tall, ginger-haired, and partially Rehnorian.

"Don't look at me like you've never seen me before," she said, dropping my hand, practically throwing it down.

"But," I somehow managed to gasp, "We're supposed to. You and I are both going to be captains."

"Who says? Just because our parents did, doesn't mean we have to follow along their path. I don't want to be a starship captain. I want to be something else. I want to go someplace I've never been." Now, she turned from me and tossed her cigarette on the ground. "It's too damn hot out here. I'm going back."

"Where?" I cried, grinding her smoldering butt into the red desert dirt.

"Back to the condo." There she was, snapping again.

"No. I mean, where will you go to school? What will you do? What do you want to be?"

"Oh." Now, she smiled for real, a smile that practically stretched across her cheeks. I realized I hadn't seen her smile like this in a very long time. "I haven't decided where I'm going to school yet, or if I even need to go to school, but I know exactly what I'm going to do." Her pony tail bobbed with excitement. Her eyes lit up as if burning with blue fire.

"What?"

"I'm going to be actress like my mother, except better. I'm not going to waste my talent turning over letters on some stupid game show."

Then, she started singing some old Broadway tune that made me want to cover my ears. She danced a little too, sort of skipping from side to side as she headed to the condo.

Kit's voice wasn't bad. Sometimes, she was pretty good, but in my opinion Broadway wasn't waiting for her. I wasn't going to tell her that though. I valued my life too much. Instead, I just followed her back inside.

#

Two years later, I found myself completely alone as I crossed the airlock into the Spaceforce Academy on Planet Mars. Sure, there were plenty of other cadets around, nearly two thousand as a matter of fact, but Kit wasn't there. It was just me for practically the first time in my life.

"You'll be fine," Grandpa Lance had said, slamming me on the back before embracing me in a hug. "I could hardly wait to get away from my family, and especially my brother, Hank."

"That's because Hank was an ass," Grandma Jill interrupted, pulling me over to her. Although her head was only slightly higher than my elbow, and I outweighed her by nearly a hundred pounds, she always made me feel like I was less than three feet tall. "You'll be fine on your own, Ary. You're one of us. You go and show them what you're made of." Then she punched me in the ribs.

"Okay," I muttered, wondering what it really was that I was made of, while Lance mumbled something about Hank and his untimely death.

Jill rolled her eyes. "You hated him while he was alive, but since he's dead he's become a saint. Goodbye sweetie. We'll see you at winter break. Don't forget to write your mom, and once in a while it would be nice if you sent a note to me."

"Yes, Grandma." I bent down and kissed her cheek, shook Lance's hand once last time, and then, shouldering my bag, I crossed the airlock to my new home.

Was I nervous? I wasn't sure. There was an odd and unsettling feeling deep inside my bones, something that wouldn't go away despite how many times I assured myself I'd be fine. If Kit was there, she'd have told me to knock it off and quit worrying about stuff I didn't know, and if I didn't, she would have bonked me on the side of my head.

Kit was always confident that she could conquer anything she tried, but she had every reason to be. She was super smart, much smarter than me. She was also better at everything, from gaming to piloting a spaceplane. Although Kyle had tried to teach us both how to fly, it came naturally to Kit, but remained almost completely elusive to me.

"Don't worry, Ary," my mom had said, after a particularly bad session in the simulator aboard the Asteroid. "It took me forever to get the hang of a small space tender. I must have simulated crashing a million times. Once, when I was at the Academy, I almost crashed for real on Deimos."

"No, you didn't, Sandy," Kyle insisted. "I remember you scoring a perfect hundred during freshman flight training. I was the one who flunked my first quarter. Ary, did I ever tell you about the time I…"

"Kyle," my mother snapped. "I think I heard you being paged. You're wanted on Deck 3." She winked at me as he ran off, a bewildered expression in his blue eyes, eyes that echoed Kit's in color and shape. "Don't worry, Ary," she continued, patting me on the back. "You'll get it. One day, you'll wake up and it'll all make sense." Then, she kissed me, standing on her tiptoes just to reach my cheek.

"Was my dad a good pilot?" I asked, before her heels settled back upon the ground and she turned away.

"Your dad?" Her face flushed red, nearly the color of our matching ginger hair.

"Yes, my dad," I repeated, rubbing it in because I was mad. I was a failed pilot and she was perfect, the captain of the ship.

"Your dad," she said again, refusing to meet my gaze. She took a deep breath. She squared her shoulders in that way she always did, as if by standing taller she stood stronger, in command. "Your dad was an excellent pilot. At one time, he was probably the best in the entire force. He was a captain unlike any other. Some said, he could have been Fleet Admiral." Then, she walked off, back to the bridge of her starship, safely locking away the memories of the guy I barely knew.

I didn't know if that made me feel better or worse. Maybe, I was hoping my dad had been a loser like me. Instead, I was alone in that distinction.

"Don't worry about it," Kit had said at the time, emerging from another simulator with what was probably a perfect score. Fortunately, she didn't show it to me. Instead, she insisted we go to the ice cream parlor on deck nine. "I'm treating today. Chocolate sundaes on me."

"Yeah right. It's always free."

"Good! Cuz, next time, you're buying."

Once I crossed the airlock and was scanned through the official Spaceforce Academy door, my name disappeared, replaced by 'Cadet'.

"Whatcha looking at, cadet?" an enormous Senior Cadet demanded, shoving all of his giant shark-like teeth in my face.

Even though I was six-foot-two, this dude made me feel as if I was half his size. Clearly, he was a Cascadian from the similarly named planet in the fourth sector. There had been several of his species serving aboard my mom's ship, and despite the fact that she was literally half their height, with just a look, she could strike terror in their souls.

Watching a Cascadian cry was a terrible thing, and something I didn't want to repeat right here. To that end, I smiled congenially and even offered a hand to shake.

"Something funny, cadet?" he demanded. "You some kind of joker?"

"I..." I began to say, noting his hand moving upwards in the general direction of my neck.

"You smiling at me?"

"No sir! That was not my intention at all." Just in case, I quickly wiped all expression off my face.

"Don't let me catch you smiling at me or anyone else," the dude growled, and then just for fun, while I was studying his face, he swung out a foot and sent me sprawling across the floor.

Lesson One learned at the Academy: Don't smile at anyone. Ever.

"Well, duh," Kit said, when I rang her later that night.

At this point, I had successfully found my bunk, my new uniform, my school tablet, and my roommate, Cadet Lester. I had lined up in my squad for first review, marched in formation, and dropped for a hundred pushups, after accidentally smiling at my squad leader, Senior Cadet Giant Cascadian.

"I wasn't trying to smile," I told Kit.

"You can't help it, Ary," she replied. "Your lips are turned up slightly at the ends. To the uninitiated, it looks like a smile. To me, it just looks like a deformity with your face."

Count on my step-sister to find a way to make me feel better.

"And, how is your school going?" I asked, while studying Lester on the bunk across the room. He had an enormous bulge on the top of his head like a giant tumor.

While Kit babbled on about Shakespeare or Broadway shows, humming some tune I was supposed to recognize, my roommate took off his shirt, exposing a bunch of those giant lumps on his torso.

"What are you, some kind of reptilian species?" I asked, recalling a Sapeosaur who had once served in the shuttle bay on my mom's ship. He had scales all down his back, and a similar lump on his head. He was a decent guy though, nice enough, until he began to shed, leaving a trail of scales and skin all over the shuttles. At that point, he was sent shore-side, much to the relief of the rest of the crew. As for me, I thought it was kind of cool. At the time, I picked up some of those discarded scales and kept them on my bedroom shelf, until my mom found them and jettisoned them out to the stars with the rest of the ship's trash.

"What are you calling me?" Kit shrieked, followed by her favorite profanity. She always thought she was so cool, so mature when she swore. Personally, I thought it made her sound exactly like a teenager trying to be hip.

"I gotta go," I said, quickly clicking off, before she either started arguing or serenading me with one of her Broadway tunes.

"Is she your girlfriend?" Lester asked, leaning across the divide to gaze at Kit's frozen image on my tablet. "What is she?"

"My step-sister, sort of. She's part-Andorian."

Kit had looked good. Happy even. Her light blue hair was short, making her eyes appear to be about twice their normal size. Even though I didn't want to, I missed her, probably more than I missed anyone else.

"What does that mean?"

"It means, her mom is Andorian from Andorus III, and her dad is something else, and by the way, he's sort of married to my mom, but not officially." Reaching up, I switched off the light, signaling to Cadet Reptile that I didn't want to chat anymore. Call time was

0500, which was only a precious five hours from now, and being a cadet had been hard work, especially on the first day.

"Does she have a boyfriend?" Lester persisted, his reading light still on. He was sitting cross-legged on his bunk, picking at a scab on his arm.

"No."

"She's hot. Do you think she'd like me?"

"Who? Kit?"

"Yeah." Finished with the scab, Lester flexed his arm and one of those bulges bulged even more. "I mean, if you introduced us and told her all sorts of good things about me?"

"Listen, dude," I said, closing my eyes and burying my face in the pillow. "I don't even know you, and so far, I don't see anything good about you. Can it until the simulated morning, bro. I need to sleep."

"I like Broadway shows too. Would you tell her that?"

"Later." I pretended to snore.

"And, Shakespeare. My favorite is Othello. Does she like Othello?"

Flipping the pillow over my head, I wondered what it would take to shut this guy up.

"King Lear is good. The first time I saw that I was twelve years old."

"Dude!" I practically screamed. "Lights out! It's simulated night!"

"I know," Lester sighed, "but, I'm reptilian. I do better in the dark. Hey, you want to play chess or something?"

I didn't respond. Instead, I pretended that I was deaf.

Lesson Two learned at the Academy: Cover your head with a pillow, snore loudly, and pretend you're deaf when you want to sleep.

The next day, Senior Cadet Cascadian guy was all over me for breathing. No matter what I did, I didn't do it right.

"Stand up straighter!" He growled. "Run faster. Push-ups with only one hand. Get your hair cut, jerkface."

"Why? I had it chopped off yesterday."

Apparently, that was considered a belligerent response to his simple request to remove the remaining millimeter of red on my head. My insolence earned me an extra hundred push-ups, a ten kilometer run, and a toothbrush to clean all the toilets in my dorm.

By the time I returned to my cell that night, it was almost simulated dawn and time to start this whole miserable process again. I was beyond exhausted, and in no mood to talk with Lizard Cadet Lester, who had developed a completely unreasonable infatuation with Kit.

"I was wondering if you would do me a favor?" he asked, oblivious to the pain and obvious fatigue on my face. In fact, he had been waiting for me, sitting on his bunk and scratching at his scabs, leaving trails of lizard skin all over our shared floor. "I recorded a song for your step-sister. Will you send it to her?"

I think I mumbled something, probably a profanity, although I couldn't say exactly what it was, as I collapsed into bed and covered my head with my pillow. I didn't have to pretend anything else as I passed out right away, only to be awoken forty-five minutes later for morning formation and cadet drill.

"Tired, punkface?" Senior Cadet Cascadian dude demanded, jogging along beside me as we circled the tubular track between the buildings. The Martian surface was entirely toxic, even to guys like Lizard Lester, so everything we did was inside, or at least I thought. "Didn't I tell you to get a haircut yesterday?"

"Yes sir. I mean, no sir. I mean, I'm not tired, and you did tell me to get a haircut, but I ran out of time, on account of the cadet's bathroom is pretty big."

"Oh." The Senior Cadet sighed, his voice filled with false sympathy. "I'm so sorry about that. I guess I had better give you something else to clean." He pointed at an upcoming window, the one we were about to jog right by, the one where Phobos was shining through. "You know, I can barely see the moonlight, on account of that window is covered in Martian dust. Tonight, after lessons and drills, you'll go clean that."

"I will?" I gulped, nearly tripping over my feet.

"Yeah, and that one too." He pointed at another window across the hall. "Actually, since you're going to be all suited up and out there anyway, do all the windows along this tube."

I wanted to protest. I wanted to scream something like, *Can't you see how exhausted I am? Don't you know, I've got homework from my classes and I'm already behind?* But, I didn't say a word. That would be totally the wrong thing to do. I'd end up having to wash the roof of this entire complex, or worse. I might even get kicked out of the Academy after only three days. That, I could never live down. My family would disown me.

Instead, I just watched him jog away, patting a few of the other guys on the back, encouraging a tiny Centipedean dude who was always falling behind.

"I don't know why he's picking on me," I texted Kit later, after I had donned a spacesuit, gathered the cleaning supplies and tethered my way outside. It was terrifying, especially when my bucket dropped into the Martian dust, sending a fresh cloud of red particles upon the windows I had just cleaned.

Now, I was heading back to my dorm room to start studying, although I didn't know how in the universe I could possibly do it when I was so beat. Frankly, I could barely move, stumbling down the hall, ready to collapse right there on the floor.

"It's because you are who you are," Kit responded to my sad lamenting text with a row of crying emojis and a breaking heart.

"Who am I? Nobody. Just Cadet Ary, a worthless bald loser who used to have ginger hair."

"No, you're not. You're the son of Captain Sandy, and the guy who was supposed to be Fleet Admiral, but bailed instead. And, your hair will grow back, although I can't imagine why you'd want it to. Oh, Ary! I'm so excited about this audition. I totally nailed it. I'm absolutely sure."

While my eyes blurred over, she continued to ramble on about the play and the part, my cell beeping almost continuously as she bombarded me with texts.

"Hey, Ary," Lester called, as soon as I shoved open the door, and fell upon the bed. "Did you think about my request?"

"What request?" I laid there in my clothes and shoes, too tired to take them off, too exhausted to begin the Basic Piloting worksheet on my tablet. It was due in only a few hours, and I hadn't read the material let alone started the problems. "I wonder how a big fat zero would look on my first grade report. I wonder how my mom might react when she sees it."

"Pretty bad," Lester replied. "Isn't your mom the famous Captain Sandy of the S/S Asteroid? And, isn't your dad the guy who—"

"Yeah, yeah," I interrupted. "That's them."

"So, about your sister, Kit, I wrote a song for her." Lester started singing something about blue hair, blue eyes, and blue roses. He might have also mentioned blue lips and blue teeth, but I wasn't sure, and I didn't want to ask him to repeat it. "Do you think she'll like it?"

"Nice, dude," I replied, mildly appreciating his singing voice. "Can you save it for later, though? I've got homework to do."

Opening the lesson on my tablet, I attempted to read. A millisecond later, I was sound asleep. Two minutes later, I was awake again, marginally refreshed considering the duration of my power nap.

"Listen, Ary," Lester began, as I again attempted to study. "I'll make you a deal. I'll do your homework if you introduce me to Kit."

Blinking my eyes, I stared across the tiny room, while wondering if I was dreaming, or hallucinating. Could it be Lester was offering me a way out of this mess?

On the positive side, I'd get my homework done and avoid that big fat zero my first week, which would probably ruin my scholastics for the entire semester. Surely, once I caught up on my sleep and worked things out with Senior Cadet Cascadian dude, I'd be able to stay on track with my classes.

On the negative side, that would be cheating, and I might get kicked out just for that.

On the additional negative side, Kit might not appreciate the introduction to Lizard boy, and I'd never hear the end of it. Next time I came to visit, she might force some drama geek girlfriend on me. Or, even worse, Kit might like him. She might even fall in love, and then I'd be stuck with Lester as a brother-in-law forever.

But, what choice did I have when every option was bad?

"Can you do it?" I handed him my tablet. "I'm already signed in. I hope you know your basic piloting."

"I'm an ace, straight A student. I've already finished my worksheet. It was totally easy."

"Thanks man." I turned my back to him and went to sleep.

Lesson Three learned at the Academy: Let your roommate do your homework when he volunteers.

The next morning, I felt marginally better having slept a grand total of five hours without interruption. Something was odd, though. Something about the Senior Cadet was strange. As I lined up for muster, he didn't look at me, let alone demand I wipe all expression off my face.

As I ran around the track, noting the new coating of red dust on the windows, the Senior Cadet was hassling another group of cadets to my rear. When I squatted and pulled up, pushed up and planked, he was yelling at a Luminerian at the end of the first row.

It was only at the end of the day, after classes, study hall, and lunch, that he finally approached me with a sickening grin upon his face.

"Cadet," he snickered, and waggled a finger in my direction, before turning on heel and marching away.

I followed, assuming that's what the waggling finger was for, only to discover Lester standing outside the Superintendent's door.

"Goodbye losers," the Senior Cadet said, grinning with all three rows of his giant shark-like teeth. Placing a paw upon my chest, he shoved me against the wall. "Three days and you're out of here. I consider that a personal best. I guess you're not going to be a captain like mummy and daddy, are you, Ginger?" He laughed and left a glob of something gross next to my feet.

"What's happening?" Lester whispered as the Senior Cadet strolled away, humming in a voice that was even more off-key than Kit's.

I didn't know, but I suspected, and was considering offing myself right then and there. It would have been easy, just open an airlock and walk outside. My dreams of success in Spaceforce were about to die anyway. Probably, my mom would disown me, and my grandparents would never speak to me again.

After that, I'd be on my own, without a family, an education, or any money to live. I'd have to find a job, or maybe, move in with Kit.

"Oh god," I groaned and mumbled my step-sister's favorite profanity.

"What are we going to do?" Lester moaned, staring at the closed door. He was shivering and scratching, leaving a trail of scales on the floor.

"I don't know," I began to say, just as the door swished open and we were ushered inside to greet the officer who was in charge of this academy.

"Cadets," he said with a giant smile plastered across his face. "I bet you're wondering why I've called you in here."

"Yes sir." Lester swallowed hard, his scaly Adam's apple bobbing up and down.

"I know of both your parents and grandparents, cadet," he turned to me, "Jill and I were students together at this very academy. Your mother attended when I was still teaching astrophysics, and of course, everyone knows about your father. I must say the apple doesn't fall far from the tree. Undoubtedly, you are bound to have an equally impressive career. In fact, based on your first assignment in Basic Piloting, I suspect you may be even smarter than your parents."

Lester blinked rapidly, while my jaw fell nearly to the floor.

"It was an exceptional performance on that worksheet. Never before have I seen so many correct answers on the first assignment. Clearly, you already know the subject matter. Therefore, I'm going to recommend you waive the course, and enroll you in Advanced Piloting instead."

"Really?" I squeaked.

"Cadet Lester, your work was equally amazing. Therefore, I'm going to recommend the same course of action for you. I'm so impressed by you, boys. Now, are you ready to fly? Report to the shuttle bay immediately. I shall look forward to watching you soar outside my window, and practice landing on that moon." The Superintendent spun around in his chair and waved at Deimos right outside.

"Yes sir," Lester and I snapped salutes and quickly crossed the room.

"Make me proud," the Superintendent added as the door swished open. "You're so like your father, Cadet Ary. He was the best. He could have been Fleet Admiral, you know, but then—." He sighed.

"Yes, sir," I mumbled, and hurried into the hall, whereupon I collapsed against the same wall the Senior Cadet had shoved me earlier.

"What are we going to do, Ary?" Lester hissed. "I can't fly. Actually, I'm scared to death of flying."

"Then, how'd you get so many questions right?" I snapped.

"I guessed."

"What? You said you were an ace! You couldn't have guessed the correct answer on every one. That's statistically impossible."

"I don't know. Maybe, I'm just lucky." Lester started scratching, while I held my head and contemplated that airlock and taking a space walk again.

"We could try flying," I considered. "I've piloted shuttles before."

"You have?"

"Well, sort of." I didn't tell him that was only in a simulator.

"We're going to die," Lester moaned and sat down on the floor.

"One way or another," I agreed. "Come on. We don't have a choice."

Ten minutes later, I sat in the pilot's seat of a trainer shuttle with Lester beside me, trembling and pale.

"You sure you know what you're doing?" he asked, picking at a scab.

"Yeah. I've done this before. Easey peasey. No problem at all."

The simulator shuttles on the S/S Asteroid were practically identical. The start-up sequence was the same. The holographic controls appeared right where they should. All I had to do now was engage thrust and move out, just as I had done a hundred times in the Sim Center.

"Hail Bay Traffic Control," I told Lester. "Request doors open and permission to leave."

"How do I do that?"

"Channel 13." I waved a finger at the Com. "Listen and learn, dude."

"Roger, Trainer Alpha. Door opening sequence in 3-2-1," they responded.

"Ary, are you sure about this?" Lester squeaked as we rose in the air, the entire universe suddenly appearing before us through the open doors.

Was I sure? No. If truth be told, I wasn't sure at all. In fact, as I slowly guided the shuttle through the bay, I considered this might be a suicide mission after all. To prove I didn't cheat on a homework assignment, when I actually did, I was going to fly a shuttle to a moon and attempt to land it.

"Ary!" Lester squealed louder, as if I hadn't heard him the first time. "Maybe, we should just turn around. I'll confess to everything. I'll say I coerced you."

"Into doing my homework?"

"I fell in love with your sister and it made me act irrational. Please Ary. I don't really want to die. Not right now anyway."

"No." I couldn't let him do that, and I couldn't stop myself. I was Cadet Ary, son of Captain Sandy and the guy who should have been Fleet Admiral, grandson of Captain Jill and Captain Lance. I had to do this. There was no turning back. There was no going home again. "What are you made of, Lester? Are you a man or a mouse?"

"I'm a lizard, sort of," he muttered, and then, closing his eyes, he collapsed in his chair. "Kill me, Ary. Just get it over with. Hit me in the head."

"We can do this, Lester," I said, my hand on the joystick, the tiny ship only a few milliseconds from blasting off this planet. Suddenly, a klaxon began to sound. If that wasn't terrifying enough, the controls on the helm flashed red. "Uh oh!"

"Ary! Turn around!"

At this point, I agreed that would be a really smart thing to do. Clearly, there was some fault with this shuttle, some problem that I was not at all equipped to handle. However, reversing was something that I had not yet learned to do.

"Trainer Alpha," Traffic Control interrupted. "You are cleared to exit the base. Move out. You are blocking incoming traffic."

"Turn around," Lester repeated.

"I can't. I don't know how." Pulling the joystick backwards didn't reverse us and neither did pushing any of the holographic buttons. "I only know how to go forward!"

"Well, then, shut the damn thing off!" Lester jumped up and reached across my lap, whereupon he yanked what turned out to be the emergency engine stop. Immediately, the shuttle plummeted to the bay floor.

While I screamed and braced for impact, the bay's alarms began to sound, and the airlock closed, locking us inside.

"Phew," Lester breathed as we sat there waiting for the bay to pressurize. In the meantime, I checked myself for broken bones or injured organs.

Other than a small cut on my lip, I was none the worse for wear, although I probably would have been better off in the hospital than whatever punishment was to come.

"How'd you know to do that?" I asked, shakily unbuckling my belt.

"It was on the homework assignment. The one from yesterday."

Lesson Four learned at the Academy: Do your homework. It might save your life.

"Ary," my mother said, glaring at me from her office aboard the S/S Asteroid. "I am so ashamed, I can't begin to tell you. You haven't even been there a week."

"I know..."

"Don't interrupt me when I speaking to you! By rights, you should be kicked out. And, you too, Lester. I've spoken to your parents and they are equally horrified." She shook her head and closed her eyes, clutching her face in her hands. "Whatever possessed you boys to do this? To lie, to cheat, TO TAKE A SPACEFORCE SHUTTLE AND CRASH IT ON THE SHUTTLE BAY FLOOR?"

"Love," Lester muttered, and proceeded to repeat the explanation about meeting Kit.

"I was tired," I muttered, as well. "The Senior Cadet made me—"

"I don't want to hear it!" my mother screamed.

"I'll take it from here, Sandy," the Superintendent interrupted, switching my mother off, leaving Lester and me to sit across from his desk, staring at a blank vid screen, and accept our fates. The Senior Cadet Cascadian dude was standing behind him, his arms crossed in front of his massive chest, and an equally massive smirk upon his face.

While I sat on my hands and prepared for the inevitable, imagining a life of roaming the streets, or living in homeless shelters, flipping burgers, or unpacking boxes in a big box store, the Superintendent reiterated our crimes, as well as possible punishments just short of execution.

"However," he said after an eternity, throwing out a word that could only mean there was a tiny smidgen of hope. "Bravery is something we commend in our cadets. Foolishness, on the other hand, we do our damnest to stamp out. The quicker we eliminate foolhardy behavior, the more successful our future officers will be. As it has only been three days, I believe there is still hope for you yet. You have been blessed with the right genetics, Cadet Ary. Don't blow it again."

"Thank you, sir," I gasped, while Lester emitted a whimpering sound.

"As for you, Cadet Lester," the Superintendent smiled, "I understand love. In fact, when I was a cadet, so many years ago, there was another cadet, a girl who set my heart aflame. I did a lot of stupid things then, things I shudder to recall, so for that reason alone, I'm going to give you another chance."

"Thank you, sir."

"Now, I'm going to remand both of you into the Senior Cadet's care. You'll do exactly what he asks of you. Obey his every command. It's your last and final chance. Don't let me down."

The Senior Cadet chuckled, a deep and unsettling sound in his throat, while Lester and I saluted and hastily made our way to the exit.

"One more thing," the Superintendent called after us, his voice taking on a whimsical tone. "Cadet Ary, would you kindly say hello to your grandmother for me."

By the time Lester and I returned to our bunks that night, it was nearly simulated dawn. The shuttle bay floor was sparkling clean. The lavatories were spotless. The windows on every floor of the building were crystal clear, completely free of dust, and every dish in the entire galley was sanitized and put away.

"Death would have been better," I mumbled, collapsing upon the bed.

"We still have homework to do," Lester replied, pulling out his tablet.

With a moan, a groan, and a host of profanities, I did the same, prepared to redo yesterday's assignment as well as today's. First, I checked my messages, though, finding a note from Kit.

"I didn't get the part," she wrote, highlighting her missive with three rows of crying emojis. "But, I love that song your roommate wrote for me. He sounds incredibly wonderful and so sweet! Tell him he's made me so happy. Tell him, I can't wait to meet him when I see you on winter break."

"You scored," I muttered to Lester, who started singing his blue love song again.

"I'm so happy, too! Just for that, I'll do both your homework assignments for you tonight."

"No thanks, bro. I've got it. I can do this all myself."

And, I did, which was the most important lesson I learned at the Academy.

Lesson Five learned at the Academy: You never know what will make someone happy, especially when it comes to your step-sister.

Lesson Six learned at the Academy: Even though you might not have all the answers, give it your best shot, because when it comes down to it, lessons are for learning.

-o-

J. Naomi Ay has been writing Scifi/fantasy for more than thirty years while suffering through her day job as an accountant and raising three amazing kids. You can read more of her work in the sixteen volume Two Moons of Rehnor series, the six volume Firesetter series, and whole bunch of short stories and novelettes that accompany both series, some of them for free.

Homepage: **www.jnaomiay.com**
Mailing list: **http://eepurl.com/bLz0lT**

The Humra

by Laura Greenwood

Braillen waited impatiently, her agitation growing by the second, and if she didn't need this job to fund her father's tinkering then she'd walk away. As much as she hated being a bounty hunter, she was good at it and it did satisfy her natural curiosity about the universe at large. On her home planet she'd only really had the old book files on her screen to entertain her and with each one she'd read, her curiosity had grown. Between her mother's death while she was still a baby, and her father's habit of spending any extra credits on materials for his inventions, bounty hunting was the only way she was ever going to be able to fulfil her dream and explore the universe. Then there was the other reason she'd started it, but she didn't like to think about that.

After a few more tense moments, relief flowed through her as a Trig male walked towards her. She reckoned that he was about six feet tall and incredibly broad, with the deep red skin and black hair that his race were known for. Braillen's relief came from the sight of the grey flight suit emblazoned with her destination's logo on the right breast pocket; so far everything was going to plan.

"You the newbie?" His voice sounded unpleasantly gravelly, setting her teeth on edge.

"Yes. I'm Braillen Smythe." She forced herself to retain an air of civility, even if he wasn't going to.

"Good. Follow me." He spun on his heels and stalked off towards the docks, leaving Braillen to follow quickly. She was a tall woman, not far off the Trig's height, and her regular training regime meant that her body was physically fit and so she had no problem keeping up with the man's brisk pace. The two of them fast approached a large but sleek looking ship, all metallic silver with the name *Humra* emblazoned on the hull alongside the same squiggly lines that were on the Trig's flight suit. Braillen knew it was the ship's logo, even if she didn't know what the symbol was; such icons were necessary in a universe where there wasn't a standardised writing system. A shiver ran down her spine; this was what she was here for. Not the ship itself but its Captain; Griffyn Anders, a man with a bounty on his head that would keep her father tinkering away for years to come.

Once on board, she was quickly hustled into a small cabin that resembled the rest of the ship. The cabin was only big enough for a small cot and a sanitiser, but then again there wasn't really any need for more than that in space. A knock sounded on the door and a pretty blonde came in before she could respond. Just looking at the woman made Braillen feel dowdy and inadequate; the woman was average height, with a perfectly proportioned body only emphasised by her grey *Humra* flightsuit. Her face was just as appealing, with a natural pout and curly hair pulled back to showcase a pair of cat-like ears. Her amber eyes also appeared cat-like, with a sparkle in them that Braillen felt herself warming to.

"Welcome to the *Humra*! I'm Kat." Her bubbly voice matched the rest of her and was surprisingly melodic, almost distracting Braillen from the woman's name for a moment.

"Cat?" She asked before she could stop herself and a wry smile twisted the other woman's lips.

"With a K. My Mum had an odd sense of humour when she named me." Her smile didn't slip and Braillen had to squash the fleeting thought that the two of them could become friends; she couldn't forget what her real purpose was. "There's something a bit different about all of us here! The Trig that brought you here? His parents called him Lucifer after an old Earth angel, but we have to call him Luc cause we already had a Fer when he arrived. And Fer... well he's one of a kind... Oh sorry I'm rambling." Kat's mile a minute speech faded and Braillen noticed she was smiling at the other woman.

"It's okay, I like hearing about the people I'm going to be working with." She sent Kat a reassuring smile while inwardly cursing herself; her original plan had been to get the Captain and cart him off before anyone even noticed that she was even there; somehow she didn't think that was going to work anymore. "So when do I get to meet the Captain?" She had to at least try to get her plan back on track. But for the first time, Kat started to look a bit uncomfortable, even causing her ears to twitch, answering Braillen's random thought about whether her ears were just aesthetic or not; it was surprisingly common for people to change how they looked now, including the addition of animal body parts. Braillen shuddered as she remembered a man who had had eagle claws implanted onto his feet.

"Erm, about that." She swallowed audibly, causing Braillen to wonder exactly what kind of man the Captain was. She'd been given a name, and the information that his family hadn't seen him in over a year, but other than that all she had to go on was her own research. She hadn't been able to turn up much on the man other than that he ran a small crew for hire, and that they were looking for a new crew member. "You can't meet the Captain until we've set sail, there's certain things about him that are... unusual."

"Unusual how?" Her curiosity spiked and now she knew that there was definitely something odd about the assignment, and despite the fact that she'd normally have dropped a risky assignment by this point, something was compelling her to keep going with it.

"I don't quite know what to tell you, we're not really supposed to tell newbies anything until we know they can be trusted." She fiddled nervously with her pistol holster as she spoke and Braillen really hoped that the thing was set to stun.

"I'm not going anywhere." Kat didn't look convinced. She sighed. "What if I tell you something about me first?"

"That could work." Braillen hesitated, unsure what was urging her on, but she found that she wanted to tell the other woman things; even things she'd never told anyone about before. Taking a steadying breath, she began.

"About ten years ago I met a man called Fyn; I didn't know his surname, or what he did for a living, but then again we were twenty, we didn't really feel the need to know, but he was handsome and charming, and oh so clever. We fell in love, or maybe lust, it's hard to say after so many years, until one morning I woke up and he wasn't there. Completely gone, no note or anything. Ever since, I've travelled the universe, but I'm tired and I'm ready to put down some roots, even if that is in a spaceship." She'd only told a small lie and that was just that Fyn hadn't been the only reason she'd wanted to travel around the universe, but she wasn't about to tell a virtual stranger that she was really a bounty hunter, or about her father. Kat frowned at her, making Braillen wonder exactly what it was that she'd said wrong.

"Come. You need to meet the Captain." Confused by the woman's sudden about turn, Braillen followed as Kat pushed the door open and walked into the labyrinth of corridors that made up the *Humra*.

Griffyn paced within his quarters knowing that he'd have to meet his new crew member soon and dreading the encounter. As much as he hated meeting new people, the crew was undermanned as it was, and to make matters worse Rykker had jumped ship. He slammed his fist into the metallic wall of his ship, angry at his former friend's mercenary attitude. He hadn't really been surprised by Rykker's desertion, but it was adding to the frustration he felt about having to explain himself to yet another crew member. He definitely wasn't sure whether he was ready to see the look of horror on a new face.

Ten years ago he'd made the biggest mistake of his life and left the woman he loved in the middle of the night to try and sell his ship so that he could stay with her. He'd been made an offer by a roaming gypsy, one with eyes and hair that swirled with various colours depending on her mood, but the offer had been for only a fraction of what the ship was worth, and at twenty he'd been an arrogant fool. He hadn't even considered the offer and had even told the gypsy woman exactly what he thought about it; that was the last thing he remembered before waking up groggy and disorientated, only to be told that he'd had a device implanted into his heart which used holographs to project him in the image of whatever the person looking feared the most. He hadn't believed the man who'd told him until he'd gone out onto the street and caused a group of local children to run away screaming.

He'd been a coward that day, unwilling to risk sending the woman he loved away screaming, and so he'd boarded his ship and flown away, eventually finding Kat, Luc, Rykker and Fer to fly with him, even if they did each see their own personal nightmares every time they looked at him. At least as far as he knew they still did.

A knock sounded at the door and he fussed about his appearance before remembering that whoever it was on the other side wouldn't see the real him anyway. "Come in!" He called out gruffly. Slowly, Kat opened the door, though he barely noticed the tiny flinch. It only took a moment for his eyes to lock on to the pretty brunette with startlingly familiar blue eyes who was standing just behind her.

"Fyn?" Her blue eyes widened in shock as she stared at him.

"Brai? Is it really you?" He wanted to pull her into his arms but settled instead for just taking her in with his eyes. While she looked older, she was still remarkably beautiful, at least to him. Her long brown hair was pulled back into a practical plait and her tall lean body was encased in a tight black flight suit devoid of any markings.

He was so occupied by taking her in that he didn't see the slap coming until he felt the sting of her hand on his cheek.

"You left me!" Her voice wasn't raised but he could still hear the anger in it.

"I'm sorry, I didn't know what else to do." He backed away slightly, unsure on the best way to deal with the woman in front of him. He still didn't know why she'd been on the space station they'd met on, nor how she'd found him now, but whatever she did meant that she could give one hell of a slap.

"And you think that's good enough? I've spent ten YEARS looking for you and where do I find you? Flying around space without a care in the world." There was no doubt in his mind that she was mad, but there was a hint of hurt in her voice too.

"Not a care in the world?" His voice was small and he threw a help-me look at Kat but she just shrugged, a look of confusion on her face.

"Well do you?" Her look said that his reason better be good.

"Yes." He pushed a hand through his thick brown hair before starting at the beginning and telling her everything that had happened since he left her.

"But I see you Fyn. You." He stared at her not understanding what she meant.

"You can only see what you fear the most." She gave a bitter laugh. "Then obviously you're what I fear the most."

She looked at him, taking in his tired grey eyes with their haunted look behind them. "For the past ten years I've been looking for you, one word and I'm yours forever, or I'll be left heartbroken."

He didn't want to believe her words were true, if they were then it not only meant that she still loved him and despite his curse she would stay with him.

"You've really spent ten years looking for me?" His disbelief showed on his face and she smiled softly in response. She placed a hand on his cheek and looked into his eyes.

"Almost every day. I've been bounty hunting." She glanced away nervous but all he did was chuckle.

"You always could take care of yourself. I could use someone like you on the crew?" He hoped she'd stay after hearing the question in his voice, but wasn't sure she would.

"On one condition; you go see your family, that way I can get your bounty too." He tweaked her nose and gave a sad smile.

"I can't let them see me like this."

"I might be able to do something about that. Remember I told you my Dad was an inventor?" He nodded, he remembered every moment with her. Hope began to well up inside him. "Well he's had some successes, I'm sure if we asked he'd look into how to counteract the implant." Rather than responding, Fyn pulled her to him and kissed her, not noticing when Kat slipped away.

Kat flopped into the chair opposite Fer and glanced at Luc who was pacing around the mess area. "So I think the Captain has a woman." Fer dropped his spoon into his bowl with a clatter and Luc stopped pacing.

"What?" The Trig grunted.

"The newbie. Turns out she was the woman he left behind. She thinks she can help him."

"I hope she can," Fer spoke wistfully. "He needs someone to stop him blaming himself so much."

"He does," Kat agreed. "She's a bounty hunter too."

"Well things are going to get fun around here!" A smile pulled at Fer's handsome face and Kat's heart beat a little faster.

"Yes they really are."

"Will you teach me how to fly it?" Braillen asked Fyn, batting her eyelashes in the hope he'd agree. He let out a hearty laugh, drawing quick looks and smiles from the other members of his crew. She was under the impression that Fyn had spent most of the past ten years brooding, and seeing him happy was a somewhat novel concept for the crew members.

"No one really flies her, Brai."

She frowned, disappointed that she couldn't fulfil her secret ambition of flying a spaceship. "Once we have some time I can take you out in one of the smaller craft though."

She beamed at him, pressing a quick kiss to his lips. "Thank you."

"You're welcome. What we do need though are the coordinates for the nearest landing pad to your father."

"I can do better than that." She leaned over to where he'd pointed to and typed in the necessary information. "These should take us right to him; it's not an official landing pad, but we do have permission to use the field behind our home if we need to." It only took a matter of hours for the *Humra* to approach her home planet, and as always, Braillen looked on in awe at the different shades of greens and blues that made up home. To say she was excited was an understatement, it had been a couple of months since she'd seen her father and while she'd sent him the credits he needed, and had one of her friends check in on him to make sure he was eating, she still worried about him.

Fyn paced backwards and forwards as Braillen's homeworld came into view. If he didn't know better then he'd say he was nervous; and not about the descent itself. He'd never met a woman's family before; up until Braillen there hadn't been anyone serious and after Braillen there hadn't been, well anyone, so it had never really been something he needed to do. Now, not only did he have to impress a man who was bound to be protective of his daughter, but he also had to prove he was worthy enough for the man to look at the implant in his heart. And to think all of this was caused by having to advertise for a new crew member! Fyn smiled to himself, pleased regardless. Whatever strange twist of fate had brought Braillen back to him, he'd be grateful for every moment he got to spend with her. He kept a watchful eye on her as they came in to land, seeing the excitement and pleasure for what they were and feeling his own emotions swell at the sight; he was never going to leave this woman behind again.

Braillen ran down the boarding ramp and out towards the dwelling that belonged to her father. It was scruffy around the edges and had definitely seen better days, but it was still home and she had warm memories of the place; that was until she saw three hulking shadows with a smaller one shivering among them. "Oi! You there, what do you think you're doing?" She stormed towards them, knowing that Fyn and the crew weren't far behind.

"Brai? What are you doing here? We thought you'd left." One of the hulking shapes, a man named Pierre who'd been trying to convince her to marry him and settle down for years.

"And now I'm back. So what are you doing?" she demanded, eyeing him menacingly.

"Your father's been talking to himself, too much time alone I imagine. I was going to take him somewhere with other people like him." Pierre's arrogant tone ruffled Braillen even more but before she could do anything Fyn stepped forward to confront the man for her. She tried to feel angry about his caveman show, but found that she really couldn't.

"I suggest you leave." His voice was low, almost a growl.

"Mama?" Pierre stammered, gaining a strange look from Braillen and a quirked eyebrow from Fyn. It took a moment for her to realise that Fyn's implant must have taken effect and that the thing Pierre was most afraid of was his own mother. She stifled a laugh. She was glad to have confirmation on Fyn's problem though, there had been a part of her that doubted him still. Her doubts weren't helped by the crew acting so normally around him despite the fact he appeared as what frightened them; while Kat, Fer and Luc had told her they saw him as a wolfman, a man made of water and, of all things, a fairy, respectively, there had still been a small part of her that doubted them.

"Go home, Pierre, and leave this man alone. For good."

She was impressed by how easily Fyn adapted to the situation and placed a supportive hand on his arm. Pierre and his friends scampered away, clearly frightened by whatever they saw when they looked at Fyn.

"Dad!" She fell to her knees beside her father and turned him over, only to find him smiling.

"Sweetheart!" His pleasure at seeing her tugged at her heartstrings, but she had to check that he was well. Before she quite knew what was happening, Fyn scooped her father up and took him into her childhood home.

"Right, let's take a look shall we." Brai's father was examining him with an odd handheld machine, the likes of which he'd never seen before. He tutted and exclaimed as he worked, but Fyn had no way of knowing what the man was on about. After bringing the man back inside his home, and being force fed some bread and butter, he'd insisted on Brai telling him everything. As Braillen had explained about his implant, Fyn had seen the man's eyes spark with interest and it had been merely minutes before he'd been pulled into another room filled with various mechanical tools. He'd seen the amused glint in Braillen's eyes as he'd followed her father and knew that he wasn't in any danger.

"Why aren't you scared of me?" Fyn asked curiously. The man looked a lot like Brai did; blue eyed with dark hair and a tall frame, and even though his hair was in disarray and there were dirt smudges all over his skin and clothes, Fyn would never have guessed that this man was old enough to be her father.

"Should I be? Brai said you only appear as what I'm most afraid of, not that you are what I'm most afraid of." He fussed some more, clicking away at his handheld. "What do you see in the mirror?" Fyn thought for a moment, he'd never given any thought as to his own reflection.

"Myself."

"Hmmm very wise." He thought for a moment, "and what does Brai see?"

"She sees me."

The man made an amused sound. "Seems my daughter is wiser still." He turned around and walked to a pile of machines, searching among it for something, though Fyn wasn't sure what. "Aha!"

"What is it?" Fyn tried to look but couldn't see what Brai's father had in his hand.

"The answer to your problem." He came back over holding a tiny box in his hand. "This contains a single nanobot designed to enter the bloodstream to seek out and destroy alien technology, all it should take is a couple of hours and the implant will be gone." Brai's father lifted Fyn's arm and swiftly made an incision. He then placed the tiny box over the cut and pressed a button which seemed to do nothing.

"Gone?"

"Gone. Now just rest here, I'll come get you when the process is over."

Braillen waited nervously for the moment her father would announce that the nanobot had done its job; she wasn't about to run away from Fyn if it didn't work, but she knew that it would mean a lot for him if it did, and for that reason alone she was nervous. Kat, Fer and Luc had come inside from the spaceship to wait as well, causing the already small dwelling to feel even smaller.

"Why don't you come with us, Mr Smythe?" Kat asked, her normal cheery disposition in place.

"Thank you for asking dear, but my work is here and a life in space wouldn't suit me." Braillen didn't hear anymore as she was distracted by Fyn coming through the door from her father's workshop, apparently too impatient to wait for someone else's say so. He looked nervous and she longed to run to him but held back. She wasn't going to be able to tell if the nanobot had done its job.

"Well I can see why my daughter likes you." Her father beamed and she let out the breath she was holding.

"It worked?" Fyn looked bewildered, almost not noticing his friends were nodding excitedly. "It worked!" He laughed, pulling Braillen to him and swinging her around in a circle. He kissed her quickly, conscious that her father was still in the room.

"Where to now?" She asked him, knowing that neither of them would do well staying on her home planet, even if that meant she had to leave her father behind. She knew he'd be happy so long as he could tinker.

"Now we go see my family. But then we have a whole universe to explore." They smiled at each other, a life of love and adventure spread out before them.

-o-

Laura Greenwood likes to write whichever weird and wonderful tale comes into her head, which makes identifying the genre difficult even for her! Her first series, Alventia, are novellas centred around Keira, aka Sleeping Beauty, and her Prince Philip, along with their allies Hansel and Gretel. It's a tale that very much told itself as she started to write it! While she's not writing, she works in Catering and is also an Assistant Brownie Guide Leader in the Midlands (UK). She likes to bake and loves to read, and like with her writing, she reads an eclectic mix of genres, and loves every minute of it!

Homepage:
http://www.authorlauragreenwood.co.uk
Mailing List:
http://www.authorlauragreenwood.co.uk/p/mailing-list-sign-up.html

The Hawk of Destiny's Fist

by James S. Aaron

The transport shuttle rocked as its thrusters made final adjustments, until the heavy vibration of the completed docking procedure thrummed in Asarik Leah's chest, signalling she had finally arrived at InquiryShip *Serens' Reach*. She sat up straighter in her seat, just missing bumping her head on the ceiling, and waited for the pilot to release the passengers. She looked around at the various people shifting in their seats, most wearing the standard Serensian blood-red duty uniform. Their collar insignia identified them as technicians or soldiers. Most would be arriving for their tours on the exploration vessel. She scanned for expressions of worry or disappointment and found only anticipation and mild boredom. She took that as a good sign.

Asarik's own collar was blank, a request from her father, Lord Robert Karak, as he had handed her the new ShipLord's insignia.

"Trust me," he'd told her, using the tight councilman's smile. "They know you're coming. Wait until you've had a chance to look around, get a sense of the ship, meet ShipLord Till. Once you put this rank on, you'll never get another chance to see the ship as everyone else does, to hear them speak the complete truth."

She had wanted to respond, "No one ever speaks the complete truth, father. We're Serensian, after all." But she didn't. There was a secret fragility in her hard father that only she seemed to recognize and dared not openly acknowledge.

If his worrying over her meant he was concerned about her assignment to the *Serens' Reach*, he didn't admit it. He had developed a nearly frantic interest in her career since her mother, ShipLord Ahsal Karak had died in combat three years ago, just as Asarik was graduating the academy and taking her first navigation assignment on *Victory's Ardor*. He wavered between extreme pride in her accomplishments and desperate worry that Asarik was following in her mother's footsteps, bound for the same end in the ongoing cold war with Gara System. His faith seemed shaken and Asarik Leah couldn't bear to see it.

"Till and your mother served together, you know," her father had told her before she left, but didn't elaborate.

The pilot released the passengers and Asarik unfastened her harness. She waited until the seats in front of her cleared, then joined the queue off the shuttle. She had to bow her head to stand, and several people shot her surprised glances. She was too tall for a Serensian woman, like her mother before her, and she wore her curly black hair short. She had her father's piercing blue eyes and people typically looked away when she met their gaze.

She didn't have a chance to note the moment she stepped on *Serens' Reach* because a business-like ensign was at the airlock, checking in the new arrivals with strict Serensian efficiency.

The ensign paused when his scan returned her name. He looked up at her with wide eyes, staring for an instant, then snapped an anxious salute. Captain Karak," he stammered. "Welcome aboard."

Asarik returned the salute. "Thank you," she said. "Will you direct me to ShipLord Till's location?"

He consulted his data pad and nodded. "The ShipLord is on the command deck, Captain."

She would go the opposite direction, then. She thanked the ensign and walked through the airlock to the corridor on the other side.

Asarik had studied the schematics of *Serens' Reach* for the last week following news of her assignment, and recognized her location immediately. They had docked near the belly of the ship, below the engines, where most cargo arrived. Father must have done her a favor and hidden her name on the manifest, which might account for the ensign's surprise. She was glad there hadn't been a greeting party.

Asarik started walking before ship's officer could accost her and drag her to the command section.

She was familiar with the general construction of the InquiryShip. It was smaller than *Victory's Ardor*, the long range CombatShip where she'd spent the last two years, but designed on the same concepts. Her gaze went immediately to small details on the walls and smooth floor that proved the crew were performing their duties to standard. The uniforms of passing crew were generally clean and worn correctly.

It wasn't her assignment to Serens' Reach that put worry in the pit of her stomach. Asarik knew the InquiryShip was a strong component of the Serensian fleet. Its long range studies of astronomical phenomena had contributed greatly to filling the gaps in scientific knowledge. What worried Asarik was her own mission on the ship: she was here to relieve ShipLord Till, take his place, and lead the ship on what her father secretly thought was a suicide mission.

Asarik spent the next hour walking the halls of the ship. She stopped at two small galleys and sampled the food. She walked anywhere she wouldn't draw attention to herself, making mental notes of any deficiencies, listening to the conversations of soldier-scientists walking by. She watched workers load cargo in the main bay. From a railing overlooking a training area, she watched a contingent of sparring security personnel as they manipulated micro-gravity with their combat interfaces, leaping off walls, flinging waves of force at each other that dented the walls. Two fought with resonance blades and their misses gouged the alloy floor.

Her anxiety shifted away from her message for ShipLord Till and focused instead on the cannonball she was about to drop in the crew's relatively peaceful, or at least dependable, lives.

Gradually, she made her way toward the command section, passing through the environmental section and the living quarters. She stopped to examine the leaves of greenery growing along the corridors, checking the plant health, and glanced in the open door of an apartment as she walked by. Everything suggested that *Serens' Reach* was ready for the mission. The only remaining issue was ShipLord Till.

She found him on the command deck, a tall, gaunt man who stood behind his two navigation lieutenants like a hammer over nails. The Hawk of *Destiny's Fist*. He noted her presence with a dull, uninterested gaze at first, ready to turn back to whatever he had been saying, until recognition snapped in his eyes, almost like surprise. His heavily wrinkled face creased in a half-smile.

"Captain Karak," he said, loudly enough to get the attention of the command deck. "Welcome to *Serens' Reach*." He turned away from the navigation section and crossed to her, extending a hand in greeting.

Asarik shook his hand, since he'd offered it first, then gave him a salute as was custom in meeting the ShipLord.

Till returned the salute, eyes still bright with the bemused surprise. He clapped her on the shoulder with a firm grip. She was nearly his height but the gesture felt paternal. Asarik felt the eyes of the command section on them.

"For a moment I thought it was your mother standing before me," he said. The edges of his lips turned down. "It pained me to learn of her death. I am sorry for your loss."

Asarik acknowledged the sentiment with a tight nod. "Thank you."

"You didn't give us the opportunity to welcome you properly," he said, still gripping her shoulder. "We'll need to complete the on-boarding ceremony and have a proper officer's mess."

Till turned to look at one of his lieutenants, ready to start barking orders. Asarik didn't want to postpone her news any longer than necessary.

"ShipLord Till," she said, making her voice formal. "I need to speak to you privately. I have a new mission from the Council."

The command deck had been quiet before as the crew watched Till greet her, judging her as well, she supposed. Now the atmosphere seemed to escape the room.

Till raised his eyebrows slightly and took his hand off her shoulder. He nodded. "Certainly, Captain Karak." He motioned toward a door to her left. "We can meet in the planning room. This way, please."

Asarik allowed herself to exhale a relieved breath and followed Till across the command deck.

#

At the doorway, as all eyes in the room continued to follow them, ShipLord Till stopped abruptly and turned to Asarik. He raised a bony finger.

"On second thought, Captain Asarik, I think you should make your announcement here." He motioned toward the twenty or so crew watching from their consoles. "There's no reason I should receive such important news before the rest of my crew. Please." The plans room door had opened automatically at his approach. Till stepped to the side so that Asarik stood framed in the opening, offering her an easy out.

"ShipLord Till," she began, not sure how to respond. Her message was for his ears, sent directly from the Council of Serens. She wasn't sure where he was going with this display, especially if he already knew what she was going to say. Till had been a savvy combat commander in his day but now he babysat an exploration vessel. His retirement should come as a relief. Especially with the mission she carried.

Till's blue eyes bored into hers. The edges of his lips might have been turned up in the slightest smile but his face was too wrinkled to know for sure.

Asarik squared her shoulders. She turned away from him to face the crew. She looked among the expectant faces. Many of them seemed only different versions of the people she had come to respect and even love on *Victory's Ardor*. She experienced a heartbeat's disorientation, overcome with the feeling that she had always been here, that they were all simply different versions of people she had known in a similar setting. Asarik steadied herself. She was the newcomer here. She was the one who had to prove herself. It was obvious now that Till was going to make her earn the transition.

Clearing her throat, she announced, "My name is Captain Asarik Leah Karak, recently of the CombatShip *Victory's Ardor*. I am here on orders from the Council of Serens to inform you of a new mission."

She met the gaze of each person watching her in turn, trying to read their expressions. Some looked expectant, others disapproving. She didn't let herself focus only those who smiled at her. She forced her gaze to take in the frowns, the closed expressions. "*Serens' Reach* has been chosen for a long range exploration mission to test the operational status of five dormant GalaxyGates."

"Which gates?" one of the navigation lieutenants asked, a woman with classically Serensian short black hair and blue eyes.

Asarik nodded. It was a reasonable question. "Kinsla, Bitralis, Halith, Llinit and Yulan Sit."

The two navigators nodded recognition as she spoke.

"This mission is a great honor for you and the rest of the crew. It reflects highly upon your efforts in the Garan conflict, your dedication as soldiers, scientists, and Serensians. You truly exemplify the ideals of Victory is Destiny."

Someone in her peripheral vision made a choked sound. Asarik ignored them. She was handing them a suicide mission and the only way to do it was wrapped in patriotism.

She glanced at Till. She was sure he knew what she was about to say next. She wondered if her father had known as well. She met his gaze but couldn't read anything in his gray eyes.

Asarik paused, offering Till the space to interject, to add anything. When he said nothing, she forged ahead. "In addition to the mission given by the Council of Serens, I am also here to announce the transition of command from ShipLord Till to myself." She let her breath out. "I will be taking command of *Serens' Reach* for this mission and the foreseeable future beyond."

There was another cough, followed by silence.

Beside her, ShipLord Till said, "Transition of command." He let the words hang in the air for a moment. "Well. I have to tell you, Captain Karak, this wasn't unexpected." He took a step back, leaning on an elbow on a nearby console. "But I've been around for a while. Maybe a little while longer than you have."

Someone snorted. Asarik didn't allow herself to take her eyes off Till. The beginning of a bead of sweat was forming at her temple, tickling. Her scalp was hot.

"And I always like to make sure I understand exactly where my orders come from." He swept a hand at the crew. "I can't command if I don't know why an order was given." He touched his chest. "If I understand an order, I'll be the first to follow it all the way to the end, Captain Karak. I'll follow it as far as is necessary. Just like your mother did at Calayis Gate. And no one will speak against any action she took, because she was justified. Justified. Though she took her crew of two hundred with her into the fire."

Till's words seemed to reach her from the end of a tunnel. Asarik did her best to ignore the sweat in her hairline now.

She would have to ignore the jab about her mother. She would have to put her emotions aside, focus on the mission she had been given. Soon all this would be over, and she would be the one in front of the crew leading them forward. Till was going to hang on until his fingers bled. She understood that. She could even respect the desire to do so. It was her job to help him let go.

"ShipLord Till," she said. "You have served faithfully and with great successes. The council strongly recognizes your sacrifices for the people of Serens System."

"The council?" Till snapped, finally showing emotion. "You mean your father, Lord Karak?"

Asarik wanted to smile but held it back. Here it was.

"My father serves the Council of Serens. This is true."

"True?" the ShipLord spat. His face was red. He straightened. "What gives him the right hand off my ship to some unqualified daughter, barely out of the academy, fresh from chasing smugglers and herding refuges? What makes you think I'll step aside and do his bidding, Captain Karak?"

"I am not here to convince you," Asarik answered. "I am here to deliver your orders. Will you obey?"

The room around them was silent. She could hear the environmental controls breathing from hidden vents.

"If you were worth a damn," Till said. "You would challenge me and earn your command. You would follow the path of Serensian honor that your generation has forgotten." He leaned forward, glaring at her. "What do you say, Captain Karak? Can you earn your command in front of the ship and its crew?"

Asarik wanted to shout at him in disgust. This show did nothing but feed his ego. She didn't need to fight him. She had been given command authority by the council. She had issued the Council's orders. He was in defiance now. How long should she let this go on?

He was an old man who had served Serens for nearly fifty years. He couldn't hope to win against her in single combat. She supposed that humoring him might appeal to the crew, help their opinion of her while she was currently an unknown quantity. She wished he hadn't mentioned her father with such vehemence.

"Fine," she said. "ShipLord Till, I challenge you for command of *Serens' Reach*. As you wish it, I comply. Single combat to submission."

"To death," he pressed.

She nearly shook her head in exasperation. His suggestion was practically illegal, upheld only by mutual agreement between combatants. She also knew every eye in the room and probably several cameras broadcasting to the rest of the ship were on her right now. If she couldn't demonstrate competence from the beginning, she would never lead them through the trials to come.

"Yes," she said. "I agree."

#

In a small chamber off the main cargo hold, Asarik sat on the smooth floor with her legs crossed, hands folded against her abdomen, preparing her thoughts. As a kind of mantra, she ran the names of the five GalaxyGates through her mind over and over again. Her mission. Her people's purpose.

Kinsla, Bitralis, Halith, Llinit and Yulan Sit.

The five dormant gates within reach of Serens System. It amazed her that once humanity had built such things. Asarik opened her eyes and looked at her hands, flexing her fingers, considering how hands like hers had manipulated the substance of the Galaxy, only to fall back into the petty wars and selfish pursuits that plagued the Known Worlds. Hands that still fought duels. She shook the thoughts away. She was Serensian. Violence was one of her many tools. She would defeat Till with her hands.

The door slid open and she looked up to find the ShipLord standing in the doorway. He stepped inside quickly and let the door close behind him. He was wearing a plain blood-red uniform and work boots.

"Asarik," he said before she could say anything, holding up a hand. "I understand why you are here, and I understand my time has come to an end with *Serens' Reach*. I simply..." He stopped himself. There was sadness in his eyes when he looked down at her. "I spoke poorly of your mother. She was an excellent officer and honorable whenever I spoke with her or observed her on duty. In fact, I have never heard anyone say an ill word of your mother. I am not pleased to be the first. I spoke out of emotion." He met her eyes again. "I ask that you forgive me."

Uncomfortable with him standing over her, even with a contrite look on his face, Asarik stood and smoothed down her uniform pants. "I believe I understand," she said.

Till's eyes flared. "Do you?"

Asarik stiffened. She raised her hands slightly, unsure what he was going to do.

The ShipLord didn't appear to notice her guarded stance. "What do you understand?" he demanded. He looked past her. "For twenty years, I was ShipLord of the *Destiny's Fist*, the finest CombatShip in the fleet. I directed the Serensian flame against our enemies. The Garans never dared to mock us so openly in the Authority's Council as they do now. I served faithfully and with honor, and when I was given this leaking sow of a science ship, I made it something to admire. Why do you think we even know of the existence of these dead gates you've been tasked to probe?" Till jabbed at his chest. "My sweat and suffering."

Asarik kept her face impassive, gauging his anger. She heard the desperation behind his words. He clenched his bony fists in front of him, knuckles swollen, as if he couldn't hold anything tight enough.

Till ran himself out of words, his eyes ticking up and down her face as if he had forgotten who she was. He blinked, gaze growing slightly dull again. "I came here to apologize," he said finally. "Not to rail against fate."

He straightened, clearing his throat. "We will duel," he said. "Hand-to-hand. No combat authority. No combat interfaces. With honor. I will lose to you, Captain Asarik Karak, and you will take my life. I command you as your ShipLord."

Asarik stared at him.

"You will do this for me," he continued. "You..." He raised a hand and let it fall as if uncertain how to speak. "You are at the beginning of your career. I see it in you." His face creased in a hard smile. "Don't think I don't see what you are, where you came from. Your task will be control of the path in front of you. Will you become your mother or your father? Or something all your own? Each path will limit your later choices, until you finally find yourself where I stand now, when you have only one choice to make, one way to control your future."

Till stared down at her, a hint of wetness in his gray eyes. "Do me this honor," he said. Somehow the words balanced evenly between command and request, speaking from one ShipLord to another.

Asarik's mind reeled, imagining herself looking through the doors he described, the distance between her mother and father. She couldn't shut out what he had said about her mother burning her crew. Asarik knew every detail of that battle. She knew her mother had made the best decisions she could in order to achieve as much of her mission as possible. She had died honorably. She had died...

Nothing changed that she had died, that one half of Asarik was gone, leaving only her distant father. She hadn't questioned her orders or the path laid out before her with command of *Serens' Reach*.

The thought flicked through her mind that Till was trying to deceive her. He wanted her to give up the command. He wanted her to question her future and go back to her father.

Till didn't know her.

"I will do as you ask," Asarik said.

#

It looked as if most of the crew was gathered in the low-ceilinged cargo hold when Asarik left the chamber. Talking and laughing stopped, leaving only the sounds of feet scraping on the floor and people shifting where they sat on piles of cargo. Heads turned to watch her cross between the stacked alloy crates. A circle of cord had been laid on the smooth floor about five meters across. Till stood just outside the circle on the far side.

Crew members moved out of her way to allow space for her to stand opposite Till. She stood with her toes pointed at the cord and took a ready stance.

"ShipLord Till," she called. Everyone in the room froze, her voice echoing off the metal walls. "I am Captain Asarik Leah Karak, formerly of *Victory's Ardor*. I arrive at the order of the Council of Serens to assume command of InquiryShip *Serens' Reach*." Her voice sounded thin to her ears. She wished she could start the speech over again but took a breath and pushed on. "By custom and right, you may challenge my orders in service of your crew who deserve only the best leadership Serens can offer. What say you?"

Till raised his chin, his gray eyes fixed on her. His voice was rich and deep as he answered, "I challenge your claim and step into the circle."

"Until one of us leaves, then," Asarik said.

"Until one of us leaves."

Asarik stepped over the cord. The room was immediately electrified, people leaning forward all around them. No doubt bets were changing hands.

Till took a deep breath and raised his hands in a ready stance.

When he didn't attack immediately, Asarik took the three steps to close the space between them. Her mind immediately fell back to the repetition of academy drills, attention focused on Till's stance, the angle of his arms, where he directed his gaze. She had fought against the hand-to-hand styles from when Till had graduated the academy. She would need to assess what he had learned since then. She would need to determine just how much speed and strength he could still bring against her.

Before she could strike him, Till straightened his right arm, clenching a fist, and announced in a clear voice, "Combat authority granted."

The space in front of his fist warped as if the air were boiling. The force from his combat interface hit her chest like a sledgehammer. Asarik struck the floor gasping, white lights bursting in her eyes.

Somewhere people were shouting and stomping their boots on crates but it all sounded muffled. She blinked as the recognition of her own activated combat interface flooded through her. Energy ran like tiny electric pins from her palm to elbow. The floor felt more solid as she became aware of nearby mass and its subtle effects on the ship's interior gravity.

Above her, Till was yelling with his fist in the air, face contorted in rage and exertion.

Asarik rolled away from his attack. His fist dented the floor where it came down. She pushed herself to her feet and crouched low, focusing on Till as he stumbled away from his overpowered swing.

The combat interface felt like a cable running from her elbow through her fist, whipping the space between her knuckles and the center of the circle. She struggled to recognize the new information flooding her body, the tiny variations in mass all around her.

As Till fought to get control of himself, she closed the space again and hit him with a straight kick. Her boot caught him in the abdomen and he doubled. He brought his arm up in time to block her fist. Force bounced off force, throwing her swing wide.

Asarik spun away. The shouts around them had gone quiet. She noted murmurs. She couldn't tell if the watching faces wanted her to lose or if they hated Till. Did they care that he had lied? They wouldn't know, of course. The combatants could set whatever rules they chose. The old man knew he couldn't beat her one-on-one, so of course he would seek an advantage. Which meant his lies went even deeper. He meant to kill her.

As the shock of his surprise attack faded, she grew more calm. She watched him move and shifted to a mindless flow, anticipating his motions and planning her own. With every change in Till, she calculated a new set of steps. She watched his hands, feet, studied the dogged intensity in his eyes.

Asarik charged forward. She feinted with another kick, forcing him to slide to her left. He tried to catch her leg but she quickly hit him with a series of small bursts of force, aiming for nerves. One of her attacks caught a pressure point mid bicep and his arm went limp.

Till crouched, protecting the arm. A wavering line filled the air in front of his interface fist as he activated a resonance blade and swung wildly. The sliver of micro-gravity gouged the floor as his fist fell too low.

Till was already breathing heavily. He tried to shake out the numbed arm as he jabbed at her with the meter-long blade. She felt the tickle of weakness in the bottom of her stomach as her interface sucked hungrily at her strength and thought she saw the same effect happening in Till. The longer he held the resonance blade to keep her away, the weaker he would become. She feinted and slid several times, using small jabs of force to keep him busy.

Growling, Till whipped his arm from the shoulder and surprised her with a wave of force that caught the side of her face. Asarik spun away, fire running from her cheek to her temple.

Catching herself at the edge of the circle, she blinked frantically. Her right eye filled with blood and tears but she couldn't pause to wipe it away. Through the haze of pain, she saw Till's knife-thin form rushing at her.

Asarik dropped her shoulder and rolled to her left side where she could still see. She came up to her knees with her fist raised in a straight-armed resonance blade, just as Till tried to shift his momentum and grapple her. He sank on the invisible blade until Asarik's knuckles hit his sternum.

Till's eyes went wide as he exhaled a hot, surprised breath on her burning cheek. His gaze met hers. His gray eyes shifted imperceptibly from anger to questioning, and then terror.

Asarik released a yell of frustration and rage. She drew her fist back slightly and pushed him off her. The blade ripped sideways, sending a spray of blood arcing away from Till's body. She stumbled to her feet as he fell back, landing on his unwounded side.

Breathing heavily, Asarik stood with her shoulders bent. She wiped her right eye, hand coming away covered in blood.

"Please," Till moaned.

Asarik lifted her head, looking among the faces of the watching crew. Their expressions had grown hard. They were Serensians, after all. They expected her to obey the law of the circle.

She squared herself on Till's gasping form. His red uniform was darker along his exposed side, soaking up blood. He looked at her for a second, gray eyes dull again, then let his head fall back so he stared at the ceiling.

Asarik formed a resonance blade. Till's Adam's Apple bobbed as he swallowed one last time. He gazed sadly, almost questioningly, at something in the ceiling, before she swept her arm up and sliced his head from his body.

Asarik released a long breath. She dismissed the resonance blade and opened her stiff hands.

Behind her, someone shouted, "Shiplord Karak!"

All around her, the crew saluted and took up the shout. Asarik wiped her bloody face again and returned the salute.

#

Asarik's new authority as ShipLord allowed her access to Till's quarters. She stood in the doorway and took in the carefully arranged furniture, a rug of Serensian grass and a few images on the walls that appeared to span his travels among the Known Worlds. Asarik stepped inside and let the door slide closed behind her.

Sitting on top of an ornate chest of drawers near the bed was a small carved box and a framed image Asarik immediately recognized as her mother. She went to the chest and picked up the image. It wasn't anything she had seen before. Ahsal had been forty when Asarik was born, so images of her as a young woman were like an unknown country. In the image, her mother looked younger than Asarik was now, gazing with amused intensity at the person capturing the moment. She was wearing a cadet's uniform.

Asarik set the frame back in its place and touched the wooden chest. Its lid was plain. The latch didn't appear to hide any unique locking mechanism and gave easily under her thumb. A spiced scent rose with the lid, revealing a stack of paper pages. She selected the first piece of yellowed paper and carried it closer to one of the wall lights. The page bore the creases of many foldings, and was covered in handwritten script that she realized was her mother's. The letter was addressed to Till.

Asarik carried the chest to the bed and sat reading through the letters, which told the story of a short love affair from her last year in the academy, when she and Till were close enough to pass each other letters written on paper. Ahsal's dreams and relentless drive shone through her words. It wasn't any surprise to Asarik when the final letter was a farewell and good luck to Till. She touched several of the words with her finger, where it looked as if the ink had smeared under drops from something wet. She had a hard time imagining Till, the Hawk of *Destiny's Fist*, shedding tears over anything.

She wondered if her father had known. Before she even finished the thought, she knew he had. Was that the reason for his extra worry? She thought of Till's face as he let his head fall back on the cargo hold floor.

Two thoughts moved through her mind: anger at Till for what he had driven her to do, followed by a small bittersweet feeling for the letters and the young woman her mother had been. She hoped Till imagined her as her mother, Ahsal, as she made the killing strike.

Asarik arranged the stack of letters and closed the chest until its latch clicked. She rose to replace the box where Till had left it on the chest of drawers. Glancing at herself in the wall mirror, she reached in her pocket for the ShipLord's rank her father had given her. She fixed the silver insignia on her collar, then briefly polished it with her sleeve. The sight of the rank made her miss her mother more than she had in the last year. She wished Ahsal was here to see her, to tell her the story in the letters from the perspective of her long life, to offer advice on the trials to come.

But that wasn't to be. She had come this far alone; she would go farther. Looking at herself wearing the rank, her sadness shifted into excitement, which she thought was what her mother would have wanted.

Asarik stood in front of the mirror with her shoulders squared, the image of her mother gazing up at her from beneath her reflection. She allowed herself a smile, then turned to leave the room and brief her new crew.

Kinsla Gate awaited them.

-o-

James S. Aaron is an Army veteran with a background in journalism. Life has led him on a weird path through mental health nursing, airspace control, security management and lately chicken wrangling. He lives in Oregon. Things he loves: Corgis, animal rescue, and Science Fiction and Fantasy from the 70s and 80s.

Homepage: **http://jamesaaron.net**
Mailing List: **http://www.jamesaaron.com/list**

Repulse

by Alasdair Shaw

"Two minutes to docking."

Commander Olivia Johnson relished another few seconds rest, then opened her eyes and leant forward to peer into the shuttle's cockpit. "Thank you, Lieutenant. It's been a smooth flight."

The pilot raised his hand in thanks.

Johnson opened up a translucent window in her inner vision, and scrolled through the standing orders she had written for her new command.

I hope Captain Jeffries won't mind that I've borrowed most of his.

"Do you think it will be bad... Ma'am?"

Johnson closed the text window and focused on the sub-lieutenant strapped into the seat on the opposite side of the hold. She'd only been vaguely aware of his presence since they'd left *Conqueror*. He must have been about sixteen, with close-cropped hair and no hint of stubble on his chin. Fresh out of Command School.

"*Repulse* took heavy damage," she said. "I don't expect it will be pretty."

The young man frowned.

"They'll have cleared away the bodies by now," Johnson said, guessing his worry. "And the badly injured have been moved to other ships."

"What happened?"

She queried his ID and a brief summary of his record appeared, floating beside his head.

"They volunteered to go in advance of the task force and nose around. When they found the Republican fleet bugging out, they realised the ships of the line wouldn't arrive in time to catch them and decided to do some damage on their own." Johnson paused and studied the boy's face. "To put it simply, Mr. Hanke, the *Repulse* is a plucky little bulldog that bit off more than it could chew."

#

"Welcome aboard the *Repulse*, Ma'am."

Johnson returned the salute from the grime-streaked marine corporal, and stepped aboard. The airlock hatch closed with a dull clank. Seconds later, the Electronic Interface System grown into her brain supplied her transfer orders to the ship's network, and status reports flooded her awareness.

"I'm sorry none of the officers are here to meet you," the marine continued, falling into step beside her. "Those who are left are too busy supervising the refit."

Johnson sighed internally, keeping her face and body neutral. "Understood. If you'd show me the way to the bridge, I'm sure the sub-lieutenant here will find his own way to his quarters..."

She'd memorised the layout on the shuttle trip over, but cycles of battle damage and repair often lead to changes.

I don't think I've ever served on a ship where the plans matched reality.

Johnson followed the corporal through the ship, pausing occasionally to exchange encouraging words with crewmembers they met. It was impossible to miss the mixture of fatigue and pride on their faces. At one intersection, Johnson stopped to examine a recent patch on the wall, tapping a few places and scratching at the edges.

Very nicely done.

Her guide stopped by a ladder recessed into the wall. "Sorry, Ma'am, but the lift's not been cleared by engineering yet."

"Not a problem, Corporal. Two floors, isn't it?"

He nodded as she grabbed hold of a rung. "At least they got the floor hatches responding to EIS again. Hand cranking them was getting rather tedious."

"Ow! Bloody thing zapped me!"

Johnson stepped off the ladder and looked around for the speaker.

"Give it here. Did you isolate the board?"

Johnson followed the voices.

"No. I thought I'd leave it connected to the eight hundred volt ring while I poked it with my little metal screwdriver."

Johnson peered round a corner. Two technicians crouched beside an open wall panel.

"You must have bridged a capacitor or something, then."

Johnson coughed.

"Go away. Can't you see..." The technician's eyes focussed on her rank slide and he jumped to his feet, nudging his colleague with his knee. "Sorry, Ma'am. Thought you were someone else, Ma'am."

The marine corporal appeared at Johnson's side, scowling.

Johnson stepped forward. "What's wrong with the board?"

The technician swallowed. "Erm, it got fried in a cascade failure when we were hit."

"We've run out of replacement boards," his colleague added. "We're trying to repair this one in situ."

"We salvaged the parts from ones we replaced," said the first technician.

Johnson crouched and inspected the damaged node. "Ever done this before?"

The technicians both shook their heads. "Not with beaten-up parts like this. They just don't want to fit."

"Pass me your screwdriver, would you?" Johnson held her hand out. "And some putty."

The corporal leant closer to Johnson. "Ma'am. I need to get you to the bridge."

"I can take a bit of time to help fix this," she replied. "There's no immediate threat with *Conqueror* standing alongside."

Two minutes later, she knelt forwards and slid the board back into place. She pressed it home with a click and passed the screwdriver back to the technician. "Connect it back to the ring, would you?"

Tell-tales illuminated the board, and Johnson eyed the flashing lights. Satisfied that the reconnection had been a success, she rocked back into a crouch.

"Thank you, Ma'am," said one of the technicians. "I think you saved us at least half an hour working that out."

"Glad I could do something useful." Johnson stood. "You should mark that for urgent replacement as soon as you get new boards. And don't let me catch you trying that trick on anything critical."

"Yes, Ma'am. No, Ma'am," they chorused.

Johnson smiled and nodded to them before turning to her escort. "Sorry about the delay. The bridge must be just down here?"

#

When she reached the bridge, it was almost deserted; two technicians worked quietly on one of the workstations, and a blonde lieutenant sat in the command chair.

"Captain on deck," barked the marine, and the lieutenant jerked upright.

"As you were," said Johnson, cursing herself for failing to pre-empt the announcement. She concentrated on the lieutenant, and details from her service record appeared in Johnson's vision.

"How's she hanging together, Lieutenant Levarsson?" she asked, motioning for the younger woman to remain seated.

"The hull's fine, we took a hit amidships from a bomb-pumped laser but that's been patched up," Levarsson replied, settling back into the chair. "Engines will hold together if we don't push 'em too hard. And we have most of our weapons back online."

"You seem to have everything under control," said Johnson. "Are you OK to finish your shift?"

Levarsson looked at her, head to one side. "You don't want to take over now?"

"You've managed without me up to now, and I could use some time to get up to speed." She turned to the marine. "Corporal, I'm sure you've got better things to do than babysitting me."

He opened his mouth as if to protest, then saluted, and left the bridge at a brisk pace. Johnson made herself walk slowly over to the captain's ready room at the side of the bridge, keeping her head up and back straight.

The moment the hatch closed, Johnson deflated. She sagged into the chair just inside the room. It was all too fast. Ten hours ago she had been the tactical officer on a battleship. Now she was the captain of her own destroyer. Her first independent command. She'd been fighting this war for almost ten years, and yet she didn't feel ready. Hundreds of crewmembers would be counting on her, and she was a fraud. She'd only got this position because so many above her had died.

#

Ten minutes later, Johnson mustered the courage to sit at the captain's desk. Her desk now. She stroked the fake wood.

Funny. I've sat on the other side of these plenty of times. Never guessed how close the walls looked from this side.

Her predecessor's effects had been boxed up and put in storage ready for forwarding to his next of kin. She logged into the terminal and, as she always did when she took a new posting, changed the default display to the feed from an external camera. The unblinking stars reassured her with their familiarity.

Johnson pulled up the duty rosters. The technicians she'd met on the way were in the middle of their third straight shift. She frowned as she opened the details. Levarsson had added a note recording that they had insisted on working through to get things done, and an order that they stand down after this shift.

She's definitely got potential.

She scanned through the surviving officers' records, noting the lack of a chief engineer.

I wonder if I can get Honeywood reassigned here?

^Ma'am? Could you come to the bridge, please.^ The message arrived directly in her consciousness through the EIS.

^On my way,^ she replied, rising and striding to the door.

"It's probably nothing," said Levarsson as Johnson approached. "But there was a slight flicker on the sensors."

Johnson sat at the tactical station and studied the lieutenant. She didn't seem the type to jump at shadows, but she did look worn out. "Could it be the repairs?"

Levarsson shook her head. "Possibly..." She looked straight at Johnson. "I know I'm not making a good first impression here, and you're probably thinking I'm all shaken up right now, but I've got a feeling about this."

Johnson took in a breath and held it. She knew that feeling. The sense that something wasn't right. You couldn't put your finger on it, couldn't give any evidence to back it up. Whatever clue had triggered the thought was too subtle to identify. She let the breath out. "OK. Sound general quarters."

Johnson opened a channel to the *Conqueror* as strapped herself into her chair. "Captain, I've taken *Repulse* to general quarters, suggest you do the same."

"What is it, Commander?" replied Captain Jeffries.

"Not sure. A hunch."

"OK. Your hunches have been right in the past, I'll go with it," said Jeffires. "You are free to manoeuvre as you see fit."

"Thank you. Johnson out." She surveyed the available weapons and checked that the manoeuvring systems had the latest structural integrity updates.

"You let him think it was your hunch," said Levarsson. Johnson couldn't tell if it was an accusation or relief.

"Captain Jeffries and I have worked together for several years. He trusts my instincts." Johnson smiled. "Besides, if it turns out to be a false alarm, this way it doesn't go against you."

"Are you sure you don't want to take the command chair?"

Johnson suppressed a shudder. "With *Repulse* as short-handed as she is, it's best if I double up on tactical. You take piloting and sensors."

Levarsson nodded. "Aye, Ma'am."

"Put some more distance between us and the battleship. Slowly, don't make it look like we're reacting to a threat. And be ready to go active on all sensors."

"Don't spook anyone. Got it," said Levarsson, keying in a set of instructions. "Which way?"

"Did you get an idea of a direction on the sensor flicker?"

Levarsson shook her head. "Sorry."

"No problem... Head roughly towards the nearest jump point, but drop low."

#

Johnson pinched the bridge of her nose and blinked hard. In another half an hour she'd have to start a rota of stand-downs across the ship; even a fresh crew couldn't remain effective if they stayed at general quarters much longer.

"There it is," said Levarsson, a note of triumph breaking through her fatigue.

Johnson shuffled upright in her seat and studied the blonde Lieutenant. "Light 'em up."

A bubble of electromagnetic waves expanded around the *Repulse*. The computer flagged eight possible targets, clustered not that far off their course. Johnson hunched over the tactical display, examining the data for hints as to what they were. The targets scattered, emitting radiation for the first time as their drives powered up.

"Republic engine signatures," Johnson announced, forgetting there wasn't a more senior officer to take her report. "Probably long-range fighters. I've sent an intercept course to the helm."

"Got it," replied Levarsson. The ship shook as she ramped up the main engines.

Johnson ran ideas through the tactical simulations. After the third attempt she banged the console with her fist. "They're too spread out. I can't even get half of them."

She caught Levarsson glancing at her, and composed herself. "We'll just have to do what we can. At least they didn't manage to sneak any closer."

Minutes later a flight of three fighters came into range. Even as railgun rounds and interceptor missiles poured from the *Repulse*, the enemy launched large missiles of their own. These accelerated hard, broadcasting signals to spoof the *Repulse's* sensors. The staccato of the point defence turrets echoed through the ship. Two missiles disappeared, but it was too late.

"All hands, brace for impact," announced Levarsson.

Johnson checked the compartments were sealed and tightened the straps on her harness. The missiles raced in. The hail of point defence fire took one down only a few hundred metres from the hull. The flash and EMP washed out the displays. Johnson took a deep breath. And nothing happened.

The sensors desaturated, and Johnson's eyes widened as she reacquired the missiles.

"*Conqueror, Repulse Actual*. You have ship-killers inbound. Transmitting data."

Johnson took a moment to examine the wider picture. All the enemy fighters had loosed their missiles at *Conqueror*. A handful were now merely smudges of rapidly expanding vapour thanks to

Repulse's barrage, the others had turned tail.

A minute later the *Conqueror* disappeared behind a glittering golden wall. The missiles ran into the battleship's flak curtain and were lost to the *Repulse's* sensors. Twelve seconds after that, the barrage petered out. The battleship looked intact.

A channel opened from the *Conqueror*. "Good call, Commander. If they'd been able to launch from closer, we wouldn't still be here."

"Thank you, Sir. It was actually Lieutenant Levarsson who spotted the glitch," replied Johnson.

"In that case, well done on backing her up, and pass on my thanks to her... I'm dispatching some shuttles to sweep likely lines of approach for any more of those. You can stand down for now."

"If it's OK with you, Sir, I'd rather go after the remaining fighters. Something must have jumped them into the system and they may lead us back to it."

The captain chuckled. "Be careful, and good hunting. Jeffries out."

Johnson turned to Levarsson. Beneath the younger woman's exhaustion, there was a glimmer of fire. "I take it you heard that? Having good instincts, and the faith to follow them, is an important part of being a successful officer. I want you to start training as the new tactical officer. I know it is usually a job for a lieutenant-commander, but I think you'll do fine."

A smile flickered across Levarsson's face.

"But for now," continued Johnson, "you look beat. Hit the sack, I have the bridge."

Levarsson nodded and rose stiffly. "You have the bridge."

With the bridge to herself, Johnson logged out of the tactical station and took the three paces to the captain's chair. She ran her fingers along the top edge, feeling the stitching, then closed her eyes for a couple of seconds. With a sigh, she eased herself down. Pride at being given the honour of command won out over the fear of letting everyone down. She could do this.

Johnson opened an internal broadcast channel. "All hands, this is the captain..."

-o-

Alasdair Shaw grew up in Lancashire, within easy reach of the Yorkshire Dales, Pennines, Lake District and Snowdonia. After stints living in Cambridge, North Wales, and the Cotswolds, he has lived in Somerset since 2002.

He has been rock climbing, mountaineering, caving, kayaking and skiing as long as he can remember. Growing up he spent most of his spare time in the hills.

Alasdair studied at the University of Cambridge, leaving in 2000 with an MA in Natural Sciences and an MSci in Experimental and Theoretical Physics. He went on to earn a PGCE, specialising in Science and Physics, from the University of Bangor. A secondary teacher for over fifteen years, he has plenty of experience communicating scientific ideas.

You can continue to follow Commander Johnson's career in the Two Democracies: Revolution series.

Homepage:
http://www.alasdairshaw.co.uk/twodemocracies
Mailing List:
http://www.alasdairshaw.co.uk/newsletter/newcomer.php

Conclusion

I hope you enjoyed this selection of stories, and that it prompted you to further explore the writing of the authors whose work was represented here.

We would all appreciate a review, though fully understand if you don't have the time.

If you particularly enjoyed it, we'd greatly appreciate a share on Facebook or a Tweet.

You can also follow the anthology series on Facebook:
https://www.facebook.com/thenewcomerscifi.

Printed in Great Britain
by Amazon

42856773R00109